# GUNSMOKE

# GUNSMOKE

### Nelson Nye

**GUNSMOKE**

First published in the UK by Nicholson and Watson

This hardback edition 2009
by BBC Audiobooks Ltd
by arrangement with
Golden West Literary Agency

ISBN 978 1 405 68266 4

British Library Cataloguing in Publication Data available.

Printed and bound in Great Britain by
CPI Antony Rowe, Chippenham and Eastbourne

## "I'M NO LIKE FOR DIE!"

"GEORGE! *George!*"

He who stood outside a door and shouted was a tall young man; a big-framed husky giant, massive of shoulder, lean of hip and long of leg. His forearms, as disclosed by shirt sleeves rolled to the elbows, were deep bronze in colour and thick with sinewy muscles. He had big hands of which he often built massive fists. He had a temper, too—though as a rule he held it under stern control.

He was clad in faded Levis, the bottoms of which were stuffed into soft-topped range boots. In hot weather and in cold his leather vest hung always open, as did the collar of his black-and-white-checked woollen shirt. About his lean-hipped waist a dark gun belt, whose loops were filled with gleaming brass-shelled cartridges, supported the scarred holster hanging low on his right thigh, snug against his leg. From its open top the smooth naked butt of a Colt's .45 protruded within ready reach of his hand.

His strong, aquiline face was clean-shaven. Red hair peeped from beneath his shoved-back, curly-brim Stetson, and there was humour ordinarily apparent in his jade-green eyes with the little laugh-wrinkles crow-footing from their corners. Yet his was a tight-lipped face, and square of chin.

The door before which he stood led off the dingy ground-floor corridor of the gaunt red-brick building known locally as "The Courthouse." This particular courthouse stood at one end of the long main street of Pecos, in the heart of the West Texas cattle country. Pecos, that sleepy little cowtown sprawled in slumbrous lethargy near the banks of a mud-brown river.

Upon the paint-scarred surface of the door itself, in small black caps was the legend:

SHERIFF'S OFFICE

"George! *Geo-r-rge!*"

From beyond the door the series of grunts, groans and salty ejaculations attesting to the fact that one Pony George Kasta was about to give birth to another of those four-line atrocities which which he pridefully labelled "poetry," abruptly ceased.

"That you, Red?"

"Yeah—that's me," Red Lawler, the youngest sheriff Reeves County had ever elected, flung open the door and went striding into his office. "For Gawd's sake, George, leave off that everlastin' caterwaulin'! Have a little consideration for the other gents that occupy this buildin'."

"Shucks," Pony George reluctantly removed his spurred boots from the sheriff's desk and regarded its proprietor with something of disgust. "Shucks," he repeated, "I'm a heap afraid, Red Lawler, you ain't got a mite o' music in yore soul. It's becomin' plainer to me every minute I associate with yuh that you got but mighty little true discernment in yore make-up. Listen:

> "A yarn I'll spin that's full of sin,
> It's a tale both old an' new——
> A saga of times when men was bad
> An' women was bold as brew!"

Lawler looked down his nose and snorted.

"Ain't that a pistol?" demanded Pony George.

"It's a cannon!" the sheriff retorted. "See that you don't turn it loose round here no more. You'll be gettin' us thrown out of the place!"

Pony George shook his grizzled head. An expression of haughty contempt stamped his dried-apple countenance. Tugging at his drooping, straw-coloured moustache he said, "The trouble with you young squirts is yuh spend too much time hellin' around, an' not a dang bit in the cultivation of the higher arts."

"The folks in this county didn't elect me sheriff so's I could spend my time cultivatin' art. I was put in this office to weed out a few of the undesirables that have been driftin' into this county in the last few months. Fellows like that Doak hombre that got himself rubbed out last week. You found out who shot him yet?"

"Wal, no—not yet. Yuh see, Red, I been right busy workin' on that new poem of mine the last coupla days——"

"Poem be damned!" Red Lawler's eyes blazed truculently. "Now you listen, George; I'm in earnest. You get busy on sheriff work an' keep busy on it from here on out, or you'll find yourself huntin' another job. We been friends for a right smart spell, but friendship an' consideration have no place when it comes to carryin' on the business of this office."

Pony George eyed his chief reproachfully. Several times he

6

opened his mouth as though to speak, but seemed to have trouble locating the words he sought.

"Gosh, Red," he mumbled at last, "I expect some careless jasper stepped on yore pet corn, didn't they? 'Pears like yuh're sorta on the peck."

Lawler's straight-line lips compressed at the corners. Thrusting a hand into his pocket he brought out a crumpled bit of paper which he slapped down on the desk in front of his eccentric deputy.

"Read that!" he growled.

Slowly Pony George smoothed the paper out. Scrawled in pencil across its wrinkled surface were the words:

"This aint no helth resort for the old fishermen
of Toyah Lake.                                        JUSTICE."

Pony George scratched his shaggy head and gave the sheriff an owlish stare.

"What the Sam Hill does that mean? Looks sorta crazy-like to me. Where'd yuh get it, anyhow?"

"The coroner took it from one of Doak's pockets last week an' has been holdin' onto it ever since."

"He has?" growled Pony George. "Some nerve! That fella's got more brass than a military band!"

"Yeah," said Lawler drily. "It's kinda strange you didn't find this note when you went through Doak's pockets. Did you *go* through 'em or was you sidetracked, wrastlin' with that damnfool poetry?"

" 'Course I went through 'em!" snapped Pony George indignantly. "Let no man ever say that Paw Kasta's youngest son was a gent tuh shirk his duty!"

Lawler snorted. "I'd give somethin' to know the reason all these strange hombres been driftin' into Reeves County all of a sudden. Reg'lar tough eggs' reunion—an' not one of 'em seems to know the others! Cussed queer! I'd give somethin' to know which one of 'em put the spot on Doak, an' why."

"Put the spot!" the chunky deputy's dried-apple countenance was wreathed in an expression of puzzlement. "What spot yuh talkin' about?"

Lawler waved an airy hand. "That's a new expression some of these city crooks been usin'. F'rinstance, if I should say 'You're the guy that put the spot on Doak,' I'd be meanin' you're the gent that killed him."

"If you sh'd say that," corrected the indignant Pony George, "you'd be a slat-bellied liar! I wasn't within miles of that fella when he got his mark rubbed out."

"Seems like all your brains runs towards poetry, George.

7

I expect you can't help bein' a little off. Who would you say *did* kill Doak?"

"Some durn gun fighter, I guess likely," Pony George showed a definite lack of interest in the late deceased.

"Gun fighter, heck! Looked more to me like some killer's work."

"What," asked Pony George, filling an evil-looking old cob pipe with tobacco, "is the diff'rence between a gun fighter an' a killer, I'd admire tuh know? They both draws their pay for the same result."

"A gun fighter," Lawler explained patiently, "is a plain cold-blooded shootin' machine—a gent that rubs you out with neither remorse nor hesitation. A killer is a man who takes pleasure in the job."

"Can't figger what makes yuh think Doak's assassin took any pleasure out of his performance."

"There were five bullets in Doak's body. Any one of 'em would have proved fatal. Besides, there was this note the coroner found in his pocket."

"Some misguided son mighta stuck that note in his pants for a joke, knowin' I'd just got done searchin' him," Pony George objected. "Anyhow, Captain Dan an' the coroner was standin' right alongside of me whilst I was searchin' the stiff. So there ain't no sense in you're tryin' tuh make out like I neglected m' duty."

"All right. But here's another thing I don't quite savvy," Lawler pointed out. "I don't sabe the meanin' of that note's reference to the fishermen of Toyah Lake. What could the killer have meant by that?"

"Still harpin' on the killer plantin' that note, are you?" Pony George made a grimace. "I can't see why yuh're tryin' to make a mystery outa the business. I don't cotton to mysteries, nohow! I got a——"

He broke off in mid-sentence. The match, with which he had been about to light his pipe, fell unheeded from his fingers.

"Say!" he exclaimed, as though struck by inspiration. "Don't yuh remember there used tuh be a outfit of stage an' bank robbers round here what was 'knowed as the Toyah Lake Gang? Sure yuh do!"

"You hintin' that the gent that wrote this note——?"

"Sure!" Pony George said eagerly.

"What happened to the gang? I 'member they got busted up, but I can't recall the circumstances. Most of their didoes was cut before I was big enough to pack man-sized boots. Did they disband, get caught, or what?"

"There was a rumour floatin' round at the time that their leader sold 'em down the river. Raine, his name was—a slick,

8

black-haired devil called 'Rowdy Joe.' He was a real card —'cordin' tuh what I've been told. He could pop a gun with either hand, or even shoot with both hands at the same time. 'Course, he didn't allus make a target, but from what I've heard he sure come close enough tuh make the devil squirm!"

"About the bust-up," Lawler prompted. "What made folks think Rowdy Joe'd caused that?"

"Wal, it was like this," Pony George said reminiscently. "Just before the gang quit operatin', seems like they'd pulled a coupla bank jobs which had netted 'em somewheres close tuh seventy thousand bucks. 'Fore a body could say *'scat!'* that pile of dinero up an' got itse'f a pair o' wings an' flew plumb away with Rowdy Joe! I expect the gang was some peeved. Things was gettin' pretty hot fer 'em about that time though, so they had tuh split up an' hunt cover."

"Rowdy Joe ever caught?"

"Not that anybody knows of. I reckon he just pocketed that money an' hopped a boat for South America. That's what I'd a done, by cripes."

"Did the sheriff's office ever get out a picture of him?"

"Hell, no! How could they? He allus wore a mask. All anybody knew about him was that he dressed sorta dudish an' had slick, heavy black hair. Big-boned, he was. Folks thought he musta been a stranger to these parts, but, shucks! any fool can guess. Rowdy Joe mighta been well-knowed around here under some other name. He might even of been a clerk in one of the banks. That gang sure knew just when tuh stop a stage."

"Doak mighta been one of the former members of the gang," Lawler mused.

"Hell! ain't that what I been tryin' tuh tell yuh?" scowled Pony George, lighting up his pipe.

Lawler's face held a thoughtful expression. His eyes had of a sudden a faraway look. "It's just barely possible," he began, when Pony George thrust up a cautioning hand.

"*Shh!* That dang' Manuel Toreva's comin' up the path. Looks like he's comin' straight fer this office," he muttered, staring out the window. "Now what in the devil does he wanta bother us fer?"

"Stick around," Lawler grinned, "an' mebbee you'll find out."

"Humph! I never did hold with Mexicans! Can't see what they wanta come to the U-nited States fer when they got a country of their own right across the border. Heck, we ain't hardly got work enough around here now haff the time for the folks what belongs here!"

"I expect Manuel considers his right here as good as

9

yours," Lawler ventured. "Seems like he's been livin' in Pecos goin' on thirty years."

"An' been in hot water more'n haff the time!"

They relapsed into silence as they heard the clump of booted feet coming down the corridor, and the rattle of dragging spurs.

A shadow momentarily darkened the doorway, then a thin wizened man with a dark leathery face adorned by a tiny black moustache stepped inside.

"*Buenas dias, senors,*" he offered with Mexican languor.

"It ain't a bad day for a fact," Lawler admitted. He gave the visitor a closer look. "Got somethin' special on your mind? Seems like you're lookin' a bit pale about the gills."

"It ees this weather, *senors*. She ees w'at you call 'thirsty,' no?"

"Give Don Manuel a glass of water, George."

Pony George, rising reluctantly, grabbed a glass and, going to the water-cooler, gave its spigot a savage jerk. He did *not*, he told himself, like Mexicans! And he was even less fond of doing chores for them. He glared reproachfully at Lawler when Toreva was not looking.

The Mexican accepted the cool water gratefully. It had a distinct alkaline taste, but he was used to such things, as are all inhabitants of the south-western desert country. When the glass was empty he set it down and, pulling a gay bandanna from his pocket, mopped his perspiring forehead. The smile he turned upon the sheriff was obviously forced.

"What's on your mind, Don Manuel?" Lawler asked again. "I don't guess you came here for a drink?"

"But no," Toreva's faint smile fled and a hunted look came into his close-set eyes. "Meester Lawler," he swept his dry lips with a pink tongue, "I am es-cared."

"Scared!" Lawler stared at the Mexican in amazement. There was certainly the look of fear on the man's swarthy features; he seemed to have taken on age while speaking. A muscle jerked in one damp cheek, a vein throbbed on his forehead.

"*Si,* as the *Senor Dios* is my witness, I am es-cared!"

Pony George scowled. Manuel Toreva had a reputation in this country of being impervious to fear. Indeed the man had always given the appearance of enjoying the hard repute with which his fellow-townsmen had saddled him.

"What's botherin' you?" Lawler asked. "What is it that you're scared of?"

Silently Toreva produced a crumpled bit of paper and passed it the sheriff. Smoothing it out, Lawler felt his pulses quicken as his glance passed over the scrawled writing.

Idling unnoticed outside the open window a man watched

10

the scene with an unholy mirth in his glinting eyes and a sardonic smile on his heavy lips.

Again Lawler stared at the scrawled words pencilled on the scrap of wrinkled paper:

> "Eight thousand bucks, left to-night by the flat
> rock out back of yore stable, will mebbe keep
> yore sinful past a secret some months longer.
> JUSTICE."

Eyes upon the sheriff, Toreva sat scowling. Pony George, too, was watching his boss. Handing him the paper, Lawler turned to the Mexican.

"Goin' to dig up the money?"

"*Sangre de Dios,* no!" Toreva snarled. "So much dinero as that I have not!"

Lawler nodded thoughtfully.

"Cripes!" muttered Pony George, passing the note back to Toreva. "Another one of them crazy 'Justice' notes! That fella's sure puttin' in some overtime. He ain't lettin' no grass grow under his feet! What's he got on you, Toreva?"

"Yes," said Lawler coldly. "What is your sinful past?"

The Mexican gave him a hard stare. Yet Lawler read a furtive, secretive gleam in his shifty eyes.

Toreva grinned abruptly. "Eef I had the dark pas' would I come to you weeth this paper?"

"That depends," said Lawler. "You're admittedly scared. *Why?* If you got nothing to hide, why worry? Just sit tight an' wait for developments."

Toreva blew his breath out in a loud *whssshh!* "Mother of God," he growled "You do not understan', *senor*. Pairhaps this hombre has the hope I weel not pay, eh? What then? He keels me for furnish w'at you call 'example' for future veectims—like maybe that Doak hombre. W'at you theenk— I'm no like for die!"

"What you better do," Lawler advised, "is to go home, lock your doors an' sit tight. So's you won't have no cause for worry, I'll have George watch your place to-night."

It came to Lawler that the sender of these 'Justice' notes very likely had a grudge against the man who received the messages. Aiming to rub them out, the fellow might take pleasure in making them sweat a little first. But why, he wondered, would anyone want to kill the little Mexican? Was Pony George right in hinting that this business might have some connection with the old Toyah Lake gang?

"Look here, Toreva," he said abruptly. "If you expect any help from the sheriff's office you'll have to come clean. Who is this gent that's signin' himself 'Justice'? I expect you've got some idea, ain't you?"

"*Carramba, no!* Eef I had any idea who this *jibaro* was, I would get hees scalp *muy pronto*. I would like for have the *Senor Caballo* keep the watch on my casa to-night."

"All right, I'll have George do his loafin' in your neighbourhood," Lawler promised. "If anyone suspicious-lookin' shows up, George'll grab 'em."

"Mebbee he weel fall es-sleep," Toreva suggested, dubiously.

"Cripes!" growled Pony George indignantly. "Some people have got more crust than a Vienna bun! If yuh're feelin' so dang' critical, fella, s'pose yuh sit up an' do the watchin' yore own self! Gosh, such gall!"


## Chapter II

### UNPLEASANT INTERLUDE


As Red Lawler, mounted on his big roan gelding, rode slowly out of Pecos along the trail to the Box Bar T, his thoughts were in a whirl. Who was this mysterious person, he wondered, who signed himself Justice? He was filled with foreboding and could not keep his mind from the puzzle for more than a few moments at a time. It was as engrossing to him as was the meaning of the sudden influx of strangers to Reeves County.

The night was cool and among the drifting shadows that hemmed him as he rode, a host of night insects made themselves manifest with steady drone, shrill squeaks, chirps and buzzings. Across his right shoulder Lawler could see a great lop-sided moon climbing the eastern sky and above his head the purple dome of heaven was alive with winking, low-hung stars that looked for all the world like tiny lanterns.

Gradually his sombre mood fell away from him and his thoughts became more natural to a youth of his years and temperament. Instead of dwelling longer on sudden death and mystery, they switched to the girl he was to see when the gelding brought him to his destination; the girl every young gent in West Texas had his eye on—the girl Red Lawler had become engaged to just three short days ago.

He touched the gelding with his spurs and the big roan quickened its pace.

For some time only the soft plopping of the pony's hoofs in the sandy trail rivalled the insects' chorus.

Presently Lawler reached a low ridge, looking down from which into a little valley he beheld the weather-whipped adobes of Captain Dan Tranton's Box Bar T. From the windows of the ranch house came the twinkle of lamplight, making cheery contrast to the long cobalt shadows thrown by the argent moon.

Nearing the ranch Lawler could hear the creaking of the windmill that reared its gaunt blades above the yard. It made an eery, disturbing sound in the vast stillness of the desert night, and was abetted by the soughing wind among the cottonwoods.

Stepping from the saddle beside the wide veranda fronting the house, Lawler wrapped the gelding's reins about one of the hand-hewn posts supporting the veranda roof. As he stepped beneath its shelter he cast a glance toward the dark outline of the bunkhouse. Evidently, he thought irrelevantly, the boys were out on the range.

His face grew sober as he recalled that this was the night Sara had set to acquaint her father with the fact of their engagement. Wondering how the Captain was going to take it, Lawler could not restrain a momentary twinge of fear. The old seadog's love and pride in the daughter whose birth had cost his wife's life was a well-known and respected thing. Every eligible cowpoke in the county was aware that in the jealousy of his love, the old boy hoped that Sara would stay single.

But he shrugged such sober thoughts away and a grin parted his lips as his big hand thumped the door. He could almost picture the joyous smile that would light up Sara's face when she saw him. She, at least, had seemed to hold——

He broke off his thoughts as he heard the sound of her approaching steps. His grin grew wide in expectancy. In a moment now she would be in his arms, he thought.

The door opened and she stood before him in the lamplight streaming from the hall. Her lithe young body was erect as a lodgepole pine and graceful as a doe's; her head, with its wavy mass of spun-gold hair, was held high. There was spirit in the curve of her chin.

But she did not smile, nor did she come to his outstretched arms.

When she saw who it was she stood quite still, one hand upflung to her breast. Her red lips parted slightly, but their parting could not be interpreted as a mark of pleasure. Her grave brown eyes held an odd, indefinable light that brought a frown to the sheriff's face.

He dropped his arms. "Why, Sara—what's wrong, hon? Ain't you glad to see me?"

If she was, she did not show it. She did nothing save con-

13

tinue her silent stare while one hand twisted nervously to a fold in her skirt.

The sheriff's voice grew suddenly husky. "Sara! Why don't you answer?"

"I—I feel so strange, Red; strange and—and frightened. I can't collect my thoughts. Red—someone tried to murder Dad!"

"What!" There was startled incredulity in the roughness of Lawler's voice. Then, "Gosh, Sara, you better quit goin' to them crazy picture shows," he chuckled. "You sure had me fightin' my hat there for a second."

"But I'm serious, Red!" Impatiently she brushed a rebellious curl from before her eyes. "Less than half an hour ago, someone lying on the hill out back fired two shots at Dad as he moved past the office window!"

"Huh?" Lawler's jaw dropped open in surprise. "You—you ain't funnin' me, are you?"

"Don't talk foolish. Of course I'm not."

The news appeared to stun him. And no wonder; no trouble worthy of the name had visited Reeves County for over fifteen years. Aside, that is, from the recent killing of the stranger, Doak.

Lawler pulled himself together. He was Reeves County's youngest sheriff—that meant something to Red Lawler. "Did the Captain call my office?"

"I don't know," Sara's dark eyes clouded and she looked away, seeming to be scanning something in her mind. "I've been too bewildered and frightened to think of anything except that attempt on Dad's life. "Why," she asked piteously, "would anyone want to kill him, Red?"

"I dunno," said Lawler. "Where is he now?"

"He's in his office, I guess. He just came in from poking around out there on the hill. He was trying to find a—a 'clue' I believe he called it."

Lawler nodded. "That's a chore for the sheriff's office," he said sternly. "I'd better talk with him right away."

He swung past her down the hall.

"Red!" she caught him by the arm; stopped him.

He turned impatiently. Looking down at her he thought he detected some sort of hurt in the expression with which she eyed him. "What is it, Sara?" he asked. "You don't want to let this thing worry you too much. He wasn't hit, was he?"

"A scratch," she said, and then—

"Red—I guess—I guess you'd better take this back." She pulled a ring slowly from the third finger of her left hand; a ring that sparkled in the yellow light—the ring he had given her three nights ago to bind their plight. "I have no right to it," she said.

14

Lawler's big frame stiffened as he stared at her astounded. "I'm serious. Please take it, Red."

"But—but good gosh, Sara——" Lawler looked at her bewilderedly. "What's come over you, honey? Is it Captain Dan? Don't he want you to get engaged to me? Is that it? Or is it this shootin' that's got you so upset?"

She returned his look silently, miserably.

"Say!" Lawler suddenly blurted. "You sure don't think it was *me* that was layin' out there on that hill with a rifle do you?"

"Of course not," she denied indignantly. "But— Oh, I can't explain, Red! We've got to break off this crazy engagement. You're too young to know what you're doing. I'm—we're—we've got to stop being silly. This can't go on."

Mechanically Lawler took the ring she was holding out to him. "Sara," he began, but—

"It's no use," she cut in. "Please don't argue, Red—" her voice broke on a sobbing note and a poignant hush fell between them. When next she spoke her tone was controlled, emotionless:

"There must be nothing further between us. You are not making enough money to support a wife as I desire to be supported. I'm serious, Red. Don't scowl at me like that." She paused, then finished, "Don't call to see me any more."

*Jilted!* the word raced through Lawler's brain in letters of fire. *Jilted!* She was throwing him down—kicking him aside like a discarded hat!

For a breathless moment he stood quite still, accusing eyes fixed hotly on the pale oval of her face as she stood with her back to the light. Then the ring he held seemed to scorch his fingers. He swore, seemed about to hurl the bauble from him—then abruptly changed his mind.

With a grim nod, his lips twisted in a bitter line, he slipped it in his pocket and strode past her down the hall toward Tranton's office.

## Chapter III

### A POINTED HINT

CAPTAIN DAN TRANTON—retired seadog an' proud of it, as he was wont to boast—though close to sixty was a man of great vitality. Though not as tall, he was every inch as broad as Lawler across the shoulders and his back was every bit as straight.

He seemed a kindly man, portly, florid and jovial. His head—save for the tiny bald spot at the back—was white as snow; a bristling mane of hair that looked never to have known the feel of a brush or comb.

He had a red, clean-shaven face whose expression was habitually pleasant. If he found the world of horses and cattle little to his liking, one would never have guessed as much by searching his large blue eyes.

His talk like himself was salty and well-sprinkled with sea-goingese. He had, so he said, retired from the sea about fifteen years ago and, after wallowing in derelict fashion about the country for some five years, had finally brought himself and daughter to port in Pecos, where he had purchased the old Box Bar T and taken to raising cattle.

When Lawler flung open his door and came striding into the room used by him for an office, Captain Dan, clad in a pair of dark blue trousers and a blue cotton shirt whose collar was eternally open, was seated behind his massive desk staring into space. He brought his eyes to sharp focus on the intruder's face and grunted.

A big lamp, bracketed to the wall above the Captain's desk, gave light; the curtains at the room's two windows were drawn to the sills, Lawler saw as Sara followed him into the office and, closing the door, leaned her willowy figure against it, watching both him and her father with nervous glance.

Lawler lost no time in coming to the point. "Sara tells me you've been shot at, Captain."

"Shot? . . . Eh? . . . Oh—ah—well, yeah. Leastways a gun went off an' broke a mite o' glass. Some playful hand with a load o' rum aboard, I make no doubt."

"Playful!" Lawler frowned. "Sara says you were hit. Hurt bad?"

"No."

"Where'd the bullets strike?"

Almost reluctantly, it seemed, the Captain shifted a stack of papers on his desk. Where they had formerly rested Lawler saw that the wood's polished surface was marred by a splintered hole. "That 'un grazed me amidships after crackin' the port lens."

Lawler, more or less familiar with his salt-water vocabulary, crossed to the left window and raised the shade. The glass had been shattered by a bullet, the bottom half, that is. On the floor beneath it lay fragments of the broken pane and one or two stains that looked like blood. There was also a darkish smear on the sill.

"You say that bullet grazed your ribs? Let's take a look."

"Belay there. It ain't nothin' to get worked up about. I'm

16

plenty seaworthy yet. Just scratched the paint a little, that's all that salvo did."

"Just the same," said Lawler, "I want to take a look." The Captain with a shrug unbuttoned his shirt. Lawler removed a bandage and made a brief examination; an ugly flesh wound, he found, but plainly nothing serious. He rebandaged it and asked Tranton to step over by the window and stand as when hit.

With a curious stare the Captain obeyed. The bandaged portion of his anatomy was squarely in line with the shattered glass and the hole in the desk.

Lawler motioned him back to his seat. "What were you doin' when the shots were fired? Seems a kind of odd place for you to be standin'."

"I'd been lookin' up a date on the calendar. The only one I got aboard is that one tacked on the bulkhead. I was standin' there givin' 'er the once over when the first gun came through the riggin' an' took me amidships. I dropped to the deck soon's I was hit. A little late," he grinned sheepishly.

"Where'd the second shot strike?" asked Lawler.

Tranton shook his head. "You got me there. I ain't been able to cross its course."

"Mean to say you don't know where it struck? Didn't you hear it?" And, as the Captain shook his head again, "Uncommon odd," Lawler muttered. "Find anything outside?"

"Well, I found a couple shells."

"Did you hear the fella leave?"

"I heard some horse hoofs a-thuddin'."

Crossing to the window Lawler stared up at the moonlit ridge. "Let's see the shells."

" 'Fraid they won't be much help. Forty-fives. I expect nearly everyone uses that calibre. I do myself," he added, patting the pistol-butt protruding from the waistband of his trousers.

"They're common, all right," Lawler admitted, but looked them over closely. No distinguishing pin marks were discernible. "Did you call my office?" he asked, dropping the shells in his pocket.

"Well—no-o. I didn't cal'late there was any sense in botherin' you boys with my troubles. I figured you probably had plenty of your own."

Lawler stood beside the desk, hands deep-thrust in his pockets. "Next time you're shot at, call my office without delay."

A cloud sailed across the Captain's glance. "Knock off, young fellow. I've been captaining my own ships too long to start in takin' orders now."

Lawler scowled. His scowl grew darker when the Captain

17

changed the subject by asking: "How d'ye like the job of bein' sheriff? Pretty soft berth, ain't it?"

Why was the Captain anxious to get off the subject of the shooting? He was, Lawler reflected grimly, acting mighty reticent about the whole affair. "You haven't given me any reason for not calling up my office yet," he reminded.

"Eh? . . . Oh! Wal," the Captain reefed his sails and came to anchor, "I'll tell you, Red. I—er—I thought you'd likely be sailin' this way to-night an' cal'lated I might's well wait an' tell you when you got here. I can't 'bide telephone. A pesky nuisance, I call 'em. I recall one time——"

"Yeah, I reckon," Lawler cut in drily. "But let's stick to this mysterious shootin'. You haven't got any enemies around here, have you?"

"Lord, no!" the Captain was emphatic. "I ain't had an enemy anyplace since the time I knocked that mutinous first mate across the head with a belayin' pin. 'Twas aboard the *Sally Schuyler*, as I recollect it, just after we'd rounded the Horn. I says to him, steppin' close, 'Mister——' "

"You told me about that mate before, Captain," Lawler's voice was cold. Lawler hated mysteries and this, he told himself, bade fair to be a night of them! First, the mystery of his broken engagement; second, the mystery of why anyone should want to kill Captain Dan; and now, the mystery of why Dan Tranton should apparently be trying to shield the sniper who had just come so close to killing him. For the captain, he sensed, either knew or guessed the would-be assassin's identity, and was plainly determined to keep it to himself.

With scowl growing steadily blacker, Lawler turned to the Captain's daughter.

"Sara, where were you when you heard the shots? You heard them, didn't you?"

"I heard them, yes. I was in the sitting-room reading. The shots seemed to come from a long way off. Probably my being on the far side of the house made it seem that way."

Lawler studied her white face, and did not like what he saw. She looked tired, haggard. He felt a wave of sympathy flow through him for her—until he recalled the matter of his spurned ring. His grim jaw hardened. "Did you hear anything else?"

"A sound as might have been made by running feet," she admitted, hesitantly.

He wondered what value to attach to that statement. Her look said she was not sure what she had heard. "Can you describe it more close?"

"A sort of fast *clump-clump* such as pounding boots might make on hard-packed earth. I got the impression that the

18

one who fired the shots might be trying to get away—only," she said, and stopped.

"Only what?" demanded Lawler impatiently.

"Only it seemed to me as though the running sound was approaching the house——"

"An' about that time," Captain Dan interrupted with a chuckle, "Sara got the notion that some fellow might have been shooting at her ol' Dad. She came running down the hall and pounded on my door." He smiled affectionately at Sara. "You ought to go to bed, ol' girl—you look like someone had dragged you through a knothole."

Lawler's glance beat hard against the Captain's as Sara said with a wan smile, "I'm all right. Just a little worried, I guess."

"Was the Captain's door locked?" Lawler asked.

"Of course," said the Captain gruffly. "I locked it quicker'n scat when I heard that runnin' bronc. I figured it was likely that careless-shooter headin' a dust cloud for distant parts. But I couldn't be sure. An' I didn't want take no chances on havin' Sara open the door an' mebbe getting hit."

Lawler said nothing. He was trying to get Sara's eye, but without success. With a muttered something under his breath, he turned his glance on the Captain. The seadog scowled. "He better do his sailin' in other waters in the future."

"An' you better keep your weather eye peeled," Lawler told him. "There's some funny things been goin' on in this county lately."

"Funny?"

"I mean uncommon queer. I don't rightly understand all I know about 'em, but I aim to before I'm through. Hard-lookin' characters have been shovin' up around here lately, an' the bulk of 'em better take to walkin' easy or I'll——"

He broke off suddenly. His intent stare was fixed squarely on the Captain's face. "Have you received any notes, either through the mail or otherwise?"

"Er . . . notes? What kind of notes?"

"Blackmail notes."

The Captain laughed and slapped his thigh. "Lord, no! They wouldn't get far tryin' that kind of game on me. What put that notion in your head, boy?"

"I was just wonderin'," Lawler evaded. "Reckon I'll be siftin' on. I got a heap of chores that sure need wranglin'."

There was a peculiar expression in the Captain's bright blue eyes. Abruptly he smiled. "No need to be puttin' off," he said, with the first real display of friendliness he had shown this evening. "Might as well sit down a——"

"Now, Dad," said Sara swiftly, "if Mr. Lawler's duties need his attention, we shouldn't try to keep him. After all, you know, he's the sheriff. I suppose he does have to work—occasionally."

Lawler stared and, staring, scowled. It had been in his mind to talk again with Sara, if he saw a chance of speaking with her alone. But after a hint like that——!

He picked up his hat and strode grimly toward the door. "I'll be sayin' good night," he gruffed as he reached it. "If you locate the place where that second bullet struck, I'll be obliged if you'll let me know."

Captain Dan looked at Sara, and from her to the sheriff. Scratching his snowy mane he said, "Sho' I'll do that, Red. G'night."

## Chapter IV

### "HE WAS KNIFED!"

A STRONG wind was springing up, a wind that sent dark masses of heavy cloud scurrying angrily across the star-flecked heavens. A surly wind that snapped and lashed and screamed. A truculent wind that drove the timid moon to cover and with guttural snarl whipped great balls of tumble-weed before it like senseless flocks of frightened sheep.

Astride the big roan gelding Sheriff Red Lawler struck out for town. Beneath the pony's hoofs the shadow-dappled plain spread vast and rolling. The trail was a dim-seen ribbon.

Riding through the wind-harried night the sheriff, like Odysseus of old, entertained many and divers thoughts—mostly bitter. The world seemed to have soured and he could see no way of sweetening it; the future lay dark as the Devil's smile across the horizon of his mind.

Who, he wondered, was the unknown sniper who had lain out on that ridge back of the Tranton ranch house and hurled rifle lead at the portly Captain? Who, indeed? And why was the Captain so determined not to divulge the fellow's identity, or his suspicions concerning that identity? Was the would-be assassin a one-time friend of his seadog days? Possibly a relative of the black sheep variety who hated to see his kin in better circumstances than he was himself? Or was the Captain's reticence simply that of a strong man treading on unfamiliar ground?

With a mind full of questions, none of which he was able to supply with an adequate answer, Red Lawler rode with a saturnine scowl on his young, bronzed face.

From time to time he glanced upward. He observed with bitter humour that the storm was sweeping nearer with alarming speed. A thick veil of scudding cloud had snuffed the moon's pale light completely. Swiftly the low-hung stars were blotted from the bowl of night. Sheet lightning showed in lurid patches.

Before the sheriff's mental vision recurringly flashed the face of Sara Tranton, pale and haggard. Almost impossible to believe the change that had come over her, he thought. But she had changed. She had discarded him three nights after acceptance—almost, it seemed, without remorse. If she had felt a wave of pity or regret it must have been but passing, for he could not ignore her pointed hint when her father had asked him to stay longer and had appeared about to insist. With the thought he jabbed the gelding savagely with his spurred heels.

The night became inky black and only the sound of the snarling wind died with the thunder and the constant roll of the pony's drumming hoofs.

Lawler pulled his slicker from behind the cantle and struggled into it without slowing pace as the first raindrops came slanting downward, stinging like bits of hail. A lightning bolt hissed down a ridge, revealing to Lawler a tree-clad rise several hundred yards to the west.

He rode with down-bent head, trying to shield his face from the blast of wind-driven rain. Icy water flowed torrent-like from his hat-brim, spilled from his slicker-clad shoulders.

Another lightning flash illumined momentarily the streaming plain. From the rise, now but a scant hundred yards away, Lawler saw a sudden jet of flame. It lanced from the dripping junipers. The report of the firearm was lost in a smashing, jarring crash of thunder.

The bullet had whined past Lawler's head so close he had heard its whisper—*"cousin!"* Under the urgent drive of spurs the gelding tore up the slope toward the ambusher's covert as Lawler's big hands dragged loose the rifle from the scabbard beneath his leg.

The junipers' dark bulk loomed empty when he reached them. Stubbornly he drove the gelding backward and forward through the slapping branches. But to no avail. The unknown sniper was gone.

Lawler pulled the pony in and sat there swearing softly. With grimly narrowed glance he probed the surrounding country as again the lightning lit it palely blue.

"Uncommon odd where——"

The sentence was never finished for, warned by that sixth sense of danger possessed by all who ride the owl-hoot trails, Lawler suddenly flung himself out flat across the gelding's neck as lead sheared past, clipping twigs from its path with

21

vicious spite. Even as he ducked, Lawler sank his spurs and the roan lunged forward with hip-jolting violence, crashed headlong through the fringe of trees and out upon its farther side and down the slippery pitch at breakneck speed.

A single glance he'd sent back and that had been enough. Four riders had been disclosed storming up the trail behind; four frantic horsemen whose rocketing mounts were slinging slime hat-high beneath the bite of quirt and spur!

Down the streaming slope went Lawler on his gelding. One stumble, one faltering step or unlucky stride and all would be forever over. But he was forced to take that chance for only Death leered grim behind.

Slime spurted like flying spray from the gelding's hammering hoofs as they left the slope and struck off across the level, swinging diagonally to regain the Pecos trail. More than once Lawler was tempted to turn and fight, but in each instance sager counsel urged him on.

Through rain-drenched murk the chase went doggedly on and on and on. The very persistence of the pursuit told the sheriff the sort of thing that would be his lot if the pursuers caught him. They were plainly bent either on his capture or his complete extermination. The wild night rang to their shouts and cursings. Lawler needed none to tell him who was that burly figure in the lead. He knew that rocky horseman well for the thief he was; tight-lipped, bottle-nosed Link Holladay—gent of easy conscience and rider of the hungry loop. Hardly two weeks past he had very nearly caught the rustler and his men with a herd of stolen cattle. But the wily Holladay had seen him coming and, abandoning his four-footed loot, had called off his men and fled. Link Holladay now was out to even up that score!

That Holladay, should he catch up with the odds in his favour thus, would kill him with neither compunction nor remorse was certain. There was not a spark of mercy in the rustler's make-up. Holladay's hate was said to be of the Indian variety and just as long-enduring. In no possible sense could Holladay be considered a sportsman. He was a man who built his own elastic code and when it proved not sufficient for his purposes he had a habit of ignoring it entirely and resorting to the long-known potency of old Judge Colt.

Again the rip and the whine of lead was singing through the night with whistling fury; dangerously close it came to Lawler lying flattened out on the running roan. With an abrupt snarl Lawler pulled the gelding in and, dropping from the saddle with bitter purpose, whipped his rifle up.

Down on the knee in the squashy slick he crouched, the long gun at his shoulder. His finger dragged its trigger back three times in swift succession. He grinned with malicious

22

pleasure when Holladay's horse went heels over head, down in an outsprawled spill. A horse to its right abruptly faltered in mid-stride, staggered and piled up in a thrashing heap as its rider vaulted clear.

Then Lawler was up in the saddle again, driving his gelding on at a hard run, grinning back at the mud-covered figure of Link Holladay. The rustler was gingerly parting himself from the spiney embrace of a prickly-pear clump where his falling horse had thrown him. As the lightning revealed him, a malignant fury was plainly discernible on his twisted features.

Lawler chuckled in better spirits. "Mebbe that'll teach them thievin' sidewinders to pull in their horns a mite," he grunted.

Glancing presently upward with his pony travelling at an easier pace he saw that the storm was passing. Blue patches of sky were beginning to show through rifts in the screen of cloud. Yet the wind blew cold with a penetrating chill that whipped his levis to his shivering legs in sodden wrinkles. With chattering teeth he pulled the slicker closer about his hunched shoulders.

As the moon peered timidly down through a crack in the scudding clouds Lawler dismissed the burly Holladay from his mind and turned his thoughts once more to Captain Dan. Was the unknown man who had to-night tried to kill the Captain the same who had levered those shots at himself from atop that tree-clad rise? If so, was it one of Holladay's bunch? Perhaps the mean-eyed Link himself?

The sheriff was forced to admit he did not know.

He thought of the hard-faced strangers who had been turning up in the vicinity of Pecos these last three months. Doak had been one, and now Doak was dead. Another called himself Buck Tawson; a third, Max Smith. Still another was known as Reede, a sallow-faced lunger whose clothes clung to his bony frame like the cast-off garments of a scarecrow. And there was still one more of these uncatalogued, loose-footed gentry; Big Ear Lester who had thrown himself up a shack near Barstow and who spent most of his time, so Lawler had heard, in shooting holes through tomato cans.

Tawson and Reede had each bought a small spread and had, apparently, settled down to the business of putting weight on scrubby herds of beef. But in the case of Tawson, anyway, Lawler knew the ranch was but a blind.

Was it one of these strangers who had settled Doak's account with five well-placed bullets through the back? If so, why? To Lawler this appeared a question that would take a deal of finding out!

Who, he wondered grimly, was the mysterious person sign-

23

ing himself "Justice?" Was he the unknown rifleman who to-night had lain upon that ridge behind Tranton's office?

Glancing across the gelding's ears Lawler saw the lights of Pecos twinkling in the distance. The rain had ceased, leaving a range refreshed and a night that was damp and chill.

Arriving in town he put up his mount at Toreva's livery stable, telling the man in charge to see that the gelding was rubbed down carefully and given a measure of oats and water. Then he turned up the street toward his office in the gaunt old red brick courthouse.

Nearing the building he saw the coroner emerge and pass down the far side of the street in the direction of a saloon known as The Merry Widow, into which he vanished as the sheriff stared.

"Now what was he doin' up here at this time of night?" Lawler muttered. He half turned to follow the man, then changed his mind and strode on toward the sheriff's office in the building from which the coroner had emerged. Though the shades of the office's two windows were drawn to the sills, he discerned that the place held a light.

Entering the courthouse, Lawler almost got himself run down by Pony George who was emerging hurriedly and swearing under his breath.

Lawler grabbed his deputy by the collar. "What's up?" he demanded gruffly.

"Up? Hell Crick is up an' about tuh leave its banks!" snapped Pony George. "Leggo my collar, dammit! I'm in a hurry!"

"I should think so. Well, you ain't goin' anyplace until I find out what's going on."

"My Gawd! Ain't you heard?" Pony George looked astounded at the sheriff's ignorance. "Hell, I s'posed 'twas all over town by now!"

"Mebbe so," said Lawler curtly, "but I been outa town. Spill it now; what's happened?"

"Been another blasted murder—that's what!"

"Another . . ." the sheriff's voice trailed off as a grim suspicion rose to mind. "Who's dead?" controlled his voice with a visible effort. "Not——?"

"Yeah—that damn Toreva! An' he had tuh git himself killed while I was settin' on his porch with a double-barrelled shotgun!"

"When did it happen?" Lawler snapped.

"Not more'n ten minutes ago——"

"Did you catch a glimpse of the killer?" Lawler broke in, cold chills running up his back.

"No, I——"

"Where was he shot?"

"He wasn't—he was knifed!"

*Chapter V*

# THE FAST WORKER

IN the sudden silence following the deputy's words, Lawler stood motionless. No least twitching muscle or change in shade of expression betrayed the turmoil of his thoughts. Motionless and stiff he stood by the open doorway, his hands deep-thrust in his pockets, staring at Pony George.

Slowly his deep-bronzed, aquiline countenance took on a harshness from inner wrath, an ominous light flared up in his jade-green eyes. "What the hell were you doin' while Toreva was gettin' killed?" A bitter quirk twisted the sheriff's lips. "Wrestlin' with that damnfool poetry, I expect."

"That ain't true," Pony George muttered sullenly. "I was sittin' on that greaser's front porch with my eyes skinned all directions an' a loaded shotgun in m' lap. What more could I do? By cripes, Lawler, I'm gettin' fed up with yore insinuations. If yuh don't like my style, there ain't nothin' tuh keep yuh from gittin' another man!"

"Pin that badge back on an' quit talkin' like a fool."

Reluctantly it seemed Pony George pinned the badge back on his greasy vest. "Wal?"

"Let's go in the office," Lawler said. "We got to talk this over," he added as he followed George down the hall. When they stepped into the sheriff's office, Lawler closed the door, walked over to his desk and dropped wearily into the chair behind it. Then he looked up. "Go on. I'm listenin'. Spill the yarn."

Biting off a generous chew of Brown's Mule, Pony George returned the remnant of the plug to his pocket, masticulated a moment in silence, then said:

"It was like this. You told tuh watch Toreva's place tonight. Not knowing what time if any, the fireworks was due tuh pop, I got over there round eight-thirty an' plunked m'self down in his best porch rocker. He set out there talkin' with me fer quite a spell. Then he knocked out his pipe an' said as how he guessed he'd be goin' inside. That was at ten o'clock.

" 'Bout fifteen minutes later I seen that big-eared jasper from over to Barstow come ridin' down the street. I kep' my eye on him till he got off his nag in front of Miguel García's place an' went inside. That was the last time I seen of him. F'r all *I* know, he may be in there yet."

25

"Well, get on with it," Lawler growled.

"Wal, another ten minutes slips by an' then along comes that lunger, Joe Reede—the fella what bought the ol' Lazy R. Like always, he reminds me of a undertaker on a picnic. Cheerful-lookin' as a quarantine fer scarlet fever. Wal, I eyed him till *he* got outa sight.

"No more passers then fer about a hour or so, I guess. Then all of a sudden like, I hears a sorta bump from inside the house. Thinks I, 'what's Manu-el up tuh?' Before that I'd heard him movin' around an' rustlin' papers an' what not. But after that bump I didn't hear a damn thing inside the house. After a spell I got sorta restless an' a bit uneasy like. So I got up an' went inside; figgered tuh swap bull awhile with the Mex.

"But the minute I hit the main room I got a shock; I knew somethin' had gone haywire right away. Yuh see, Manu-el an' me had agreed tuh leave the livin' room lamp burnin'. When I got there it was out.

"I felt around till I found the lamp—then I got another shock. It was still hot! I waited a bit, then whispered Manu-el's name. No answer. Then I called him—kinda loud, like yuh'd call a hawg. Only answer I got was from the echoes. That place gives me the creeps an' I ain't kiddin' yuh. Everytime yuh speak a dang echo plops yore talk right back at yuh. It ain't the sorta thing which makes a nervous gent like me feel comfortable. When I says 'Manu-el! back comes that blasted echo—Man-u-el-l-l!' "

Pony George paused to wipe his forehead.

"Wal, I finally got a match scratched somehow an' lit the lamp. When I turned round tuh get a good look at the place the shotgun dang nigh dropped from m' hands! There was that cussed greaser settin' right behind me all the time an' he'd never let out a peep. If he'd a laughed then, I'd a brained him. But right now," Pony George sighed, "I wish he had. He never batted a eye an' pretty soon I noticed as how he was hunched forward kinda odd. I moved closer an' right then yuh coulda sold ol' man Kasta's little son George fer less than a nickel. There was a knife stuck in Toreva's throat hilt-deep an' blood all over 'im!"

There was a hard glint to Lawler's eyes. "I reckon you put that knife where it won't get lost. Handle it careful, did you, so's not to obliterate fingerprints?"

Tony George looked reproachful. "Could yuh ask me such a question? Naturally I took good care o' that blade. I jest got done lockin' it up in yore desk when yuh stopped me in the corridor. Here's yore key," he tossed it on the desk.

Toying with it absently, Lawler asked:

"Any sign of the killer? Any clues other than the knife?"

"Just this," Pony George grunted, and dropped a crumpled bit of paper in the sheriff's outstretched hand. "It was tied around the haft of the knife with a hunk of string."

Spreading the crumpled paper out with some trepidation, Lawler read:

"Tally two for Justice!"

"So he's at it again!" Lawler's voice was harsh with anger. "I've had about enough of this. Somebody will wish they'd never heard of Reeves County time I get through with 'em!"

There was stillness for a space then. Lawler's brooding eyes were fixed unseeingly on the killer's note. His face was like a mask in its absence of mobility. After a bit he sighed, then looking up he asked, "What time's Kringle aimin' to have the inquest?"

"Nine o'clock. To-morrow mornin', he said."

Nodding, the sheriff picked up the key. "Which drawer?"

"Top left."

Starting to insert the key in the drawer mentioned, Lawler abruptly tensed. With his left hand he reached abruptly out and yanked the drawer open without use of the key in his right. "This lock is broken, George. Was it all right when you put the knife in here?"

"How could I have locked it if it wasn't?" countered Pony George, eyeing Lawler curiously. "Broken, eh? Wal, if it is, whoever broke it must have been a dang fast worker, 'cause he'd of had tuh do it while me an' you was talkin' in the corridor——"

Lawler's cold drawl cut in upon George's rambling. "He's a fast worker, all right—too damned fast by far! He's got his knife back. This drawer's empty as last year's sunflowers. We might's well go home an' get to bed."

## Chapter VI

### "HE'S MEANER'N GAR SOUP!"

HAVING just finished an early breakfast, Red Lawler sauntered up the street to the courthouse, threw away his toothpick and entered the long ground-floor corridor. The first, loudest and *only* thing he heard for several moments was the voice of Pony George. Never a thing to brag about, at this instant it was raised on high in a most dismal yammer—a sound strangely reminiscent of the noise coyotes make when baying at the moon.

Lawler paused to listen:

> "——a breeze about Kyote Cal,
> A low-down son of Hell——
> A story about a gal named Lou,
> Who laffed when Kyote fell!"

Lawler's suspicions had been verified; this was more of his deputy's damnfool ballading. With a grimace he reached out to open the door. Pony George sang dolefully on:

> "This ornery Cal was the sneakin' pal
> What stole his pard's best dame;
> She was a busy, hystlin' skirt
> Thet sang in the Golden Flame."

Flinging open the door Lawler stood regarding his deputy with a dark scowl. Pony George was sprawled contortionistically in the sheriff's swivel chair with his spurred heels resting on the sheriff's desk. It was the deputy's favourite posture—when Lawler was not around.

Gripped firmly in one hand the poetic Pony George held a pad of paper, balancing it on his knee. In the other hand, gripped with equal firmness, was a stub of pencil. Hearing the opening of the door, George said without looking up:

"This here ballad of mine is gonna be a sure-enough world-beater. Listen at this, Gracie——"

> "Now the snappiest gal in the Golden Flame
> Was the dame thet was knowed as Lou——
> A creation of times when guns was law,
> An' women was fast an' few!"

He looked up in grinning expectancy of "Gracie's" approval. The grin went lop-sided when he saw the scowling Lawler. His face fell like a sponge-cake in a winter gale.

Arms akimbo the sheriff stared. He looked mad, yet was hard put to restrain a chuckle at sight of the comic expression stamping Pony George's dried-apple countenance.

"Wal!" said Pony George defiantly. "Go ahead—say it!"

"Who's Gracie?"

"None of yore dang never-mind," snapped Pony George, and took his spurred heels from the sheriff's desk. Then, realizing that no fireworks had exploded, he ventured hesitantly:

"How'd it sound?"

28

"Terrible," said Lawler with brutal frankness. "You aren't much better poet than you are a deputy sheriff. 'F I was you, I'd find some other way to occupy my time."

Pony George sniffed. "The rewards o' labour," he said loftily, "are notoriously meagre." Putting away his pad and pencil stub he began a conscientious searching of his pockets, each and every, with great show of growing wonder.

"Here," Lawler grunted, and tossed his sack of Durham into the deputy's lap.

With a sigh Pony George got out his corncob pipe and filled it generously with the sheriff's tobacco.

"Never mind puttin' the rest in your pocket, George. I got a pipe, too," Lawler reminded.

"Durham," said Pony George musingly. "Not so bad," he added with the air of a connoisseur, "but tobacco as a whole ain't up tuh what it used to be. An' they're chargin' more'n ever. I can't figger what this country's comin' to, what with the high cost o' livin', the disgraceful size o' wages an' the suddenness of death. I——"

"Yeah, deputies don't get a whale of a big salary," remarked Lawler drily. "Still, I expect I could get another one all right, if you're thinkin' of handin' in your star."

"What happened out tuh Tranton's las' night?" Pony George abruptly changed the subject. "See Sara? What'd the ol' man say when yuh popped the question?"

Lawler scowled. "I didn't pop it. Somebody took a coupla shots at the Captain from the ridge out back of his office."

"Miss him?"

"One of 'em did. The other took a little skin off his ribs."

"This country is headin' for hell. Gettin' so a fella ain't safe nowheres!"

Briefly Lawler went over the incidents of the previous evening, up until the time he'd left the Box Bar T.

"You called the turn, Red," Pony George admitted. "We got three mysteries tuh solve. First, the mystery of why any gent would wanta shoot Dan Tranton; second, the question o' why Sara went an' busted yore engagement; an' third, the mystery of why the Captain's tryin' tuh shield the skunk that nearly potted him."

"But from the standpoint of this office," added Lawler slowly, "the most important question we've got to answer is, who is this unknown killer who's signin' himself 'Justice'?"

Pony George nodded. "Far as yore busted engagement is concerned—wal, tuh my way o' thinkin', it's jest a case o' the well-knowed female temperament. Yuh can't never tell what a male of a woman's gonna do next. Downright unreliable—both of 'em!"

Lawler was not paying much attention to his deputy's

29

chatter. He was finding that thinking came hard this morning. Sara Tranton's oval face and golden hair kept so scattering his thoughts as soon as formulated. No plausible reason could he think of to account for that broken engagement. The Captain, he reflected, must have kicked. That hurt a bit, too. For he and the Captain had always gotten along well.

If Sara had been merely exercising a woman's prerogative —the right to change her mind—he told himself she was not worth another thought. But he continued thinking about her, nevertheless, and his thoughts were both confused and painful.

He swore beneath his breath. This would never do—he had his job to think about, and just now that job was big enough to take up all this time. The inquest on Toreva was scheduled for nine o'clock. It was eight-twenty now.

"Somebody sure seems hell-bent on c'ralin' himself some notches," Pony George was saying. "It's gettin' so I count ten ever' time I step outside this office. If 'twas anyone but you that was sheriffin' this county, I'd quit in a minute."

"I don't expect you need to worry, George. You're too small fry."

Pony George was not offended. "Lightnin's been knowed tuh strike in some mighty strange places," he said seriously. "Figger it was Justice tried tuh get old Tranton?"

"Couldn't say. I tell you, George, this is the most tangled-up damn' mess I ever been in. Why should all these strangers pile up around this country?"

"Ah," sighed Pony George, "if we knew that, we'd know somethin' sure enough."

"Humph! If one of these strangers is doin' the killin's he must be settlin' some old grudge, way I look at it. But why here an' now?" demanded Lawler as, with hands deep-thrust in pockets, he paced the floor. "Few people nurse a grudge over a period of years. Doak was a stranger, but Manuel Toreva lived in Pecos dang near all his life. I tell you, this business has got me fightin' my hat, got my nerves to janglin' so I can't keep still."

"I seen where they're advertisin' some kinda stuff in the papers what they claim's good for raw nerves. Believe it's called 'Merkel's Oxidine Bitters'——"

The sudden shrilling of the telephone drowned the rest of the deputy's words. Scooping the receiver to his ear, Pony George said "Hah?" and handed the instrument to Lawler. "Fer you, Red. Sounds like Captain Dan."

"Hello," said Lawler gruffly. "That you, Captain? . . . Yeah. . . . Oh! . . . Where'd you get that notion? . . . Uh-huh. Well, all right. I'll look into it. Much obliged." There was a puzzled expression on his youthful face as he hung up.

"What'd he want?"

"Claimed that after thinkin' things over last night, he's come to the conclusion it was Tawson who took them shots at him."

"Tawson!" Pony George looked startled. Then abruptly he laughed. "Can't yuh jest picture ol' Buck Tawson, U.S. Marshal, layin' belly-down on that ridge a-workin' the lever of a rifle? We oughta tell Tawson—by cripes, that's the best one I ever heard on him!"

Lawler's answer was thoughtful. "But the Captain doesn't know that Tawson's a Federal officer. Like the rest of the folks around here, Tranton likely figures Tawson for a reg'lar small-spread cowman——"

"Comes tuh that," Pony George broke in, *"we* don't *know* that Tawson is a Federal officer. We're jest takin' his word fer it on the strength of his pryin' an' snoopin' an' that badge he's totin' round. Which, when yuh come tuh boil 'er down, don't mean no more'n a hill o' beans." Pony George held no high regard for Federal Agents, and took no shame in saying so.

"I reckon he's a marshal," Lawler said. "He's a newcomer, though, an' likely the Captain——"

"Speakin' o' newcomers," Pony George broke in, "Buck Tawson ain't the only pilgrim tuh like the Pecos climate. There's that walkin' corpse—Joe Reede, what owns the Lazy R. An' that big-eared jasper, Lester, which has bedded down over near Barstow. An' Link Holladay, the damn' rustler—they're all fairly recent importations."

"You're right," Lawler admitted. "It's a wonder the Captain didn't happen to pick on one of them if he's tryin' to throw us off the track. Somehow I got a hunch he knows who the fella is. An' I don't think it was Buck Tawson—do you?"

Pony George sniffed, took the other side of the argument:

"Yuh can't never tell, Red, what them dang Federal agents is apt tuh do. I've knowed some mighty ornery marshals in my time. Worse'n a skittish woman, they are. If Tawson's taken a dislike tuh Captain Dan, I wouldn't put it past the black-faced polecat tuh take a rifle an' lay for him!"

"Black-faced?"

"Wal, mebbe Mexicans is darker—but dang little. He's a sight too dark for me. He's got a pan like a chunk of ol' mahogany. Yeah, an' a mean eye, too."

"I expect his feelin's might be aggravated if he heard you say that, George."

"Hell! A marshal ain't got no feelin's—he'd eat off the same plate with a snake! I wouldn't trust one of 'em farther'n I c'ld sling a hoss by the tail!"

Lawler grinned. He did not attach a great deal of weight

31

to Pony George's opinions—particularly his opinions concerning government officers. Such an officer had once had occasion to hale the deputy into court for running an illicit whisky plant and Pony George's views had become a little warped by the experience.

Tawson, as the Reeves County Sheriff's Office had good cause to know, was a U.S. Marshal detailed to Pecos to investigate an anonymous tip suggesting that members of the old Toyah Lake gang might there be located.

This much, and this much only, had the reticent Tawson confided. Using the tumbledown old Bar 2 for a smoke screen, he was posing as a small-spread rancher.

Both Lawler and his deputy, having been born and raised in the vicinity, had heard plenty of colourful yarns about the former Toyah Lake gang. Their specialty had been the robbing of stages, with an occasional bank robbery and killing thrown in to make the business interesting. Their fame was almost legendary—an ill-starred repute highly unsavoury to the honest folk who had been rearing families in the vicinity of the gang's former outrages.

"Any of that bunch ever caught?" Lawler asked abruptly.

"One," said Pony George. "I 'member thinkin' 'twas kinda tough on him, bein' as the others got off scot-free."

"Convicted?"

"I'll say he was! Folks was so glad tuh git their hands on one of that gang they insisted on makin' a example outa him." Pony George knocked the ashes from his pipe. "He was sent up in '20 an' s' far as I know, he's still up! Give his name as Tim Rein—though some folks figgered at the time he mighta been Rowdy Joe himself."

"You told me yesterday," Lawler objected, "that Rowdy Joe skipped off with the swag taken in by the gang on their last two jobs."

"That's so. But this here fella was caught an' sentenced before the gang broke up. That other rumour hadn't got started then. I tell yuh, hellin' around jest don't pay no more—not less'n yuh're king-pin of the gang."

Beside the desk Lawler stood, hands deep-thrust in his pockets, his green eyes brooding on the drawer's broken lock.

"I wonder," he said slowly, musingly, as though speaking his thoughts aloud, "if Captain Dan could ever have been mixed up with that gang?"

Pony George eyed him in surprise. "Don't see how. Shucks, he was out on the boundin' waves when that bunch was hellin' round this country. He never even showed here till five years after the gang broke up."

"I reckon it mebbe was this justice gent which took them shots at him last night."

"Wal, it don't look like tuh me that that would connect Tranton with the gang."

"You remember," said Lawler, "that in one of his notes, the killer mentions the unhealthy state of this climate for the 'old fishermen of Toyah Lake.' I'm bettin' large you were right about that meaning Rowdy Joe's gang."

"Wal, speakin' personal-like, the whole thing's a crazy jumble anyhow. Gosh, I jest thought up a new verse for m' Ballad of Kyote Cal—the mos' dangerous man since Billy the Kid. Listen at it:

"She was born in the night: by the night she lived,
     But thet's aside o' the point——
     She lured the crowd of drink-crazed lads
     Thet flocked tuh the Golden joint."

The dried-apple countenance of Pony George expanded in grinning pride. "Ain't that a honey!"

"It's an atrocity," said Lawler, and changed the subject. "The gent that stole the fatal weapon out of this drawer is nobody's fool. An' he was long on guts. Remember, we were standin' right outside the door practically when he must have slipped in through one of these open windows.

"Then he broke open the desk drawer, closed it an' slid outa the office without us even suspectin' anyone had been in it. That's pretty slick. How long you figure you were outside the office before we went back in?"

"Not more than three minutes at the outside."

"That fellow's not only nervy, he's clever an' fast——"

"Fast!" Pony George snorted. "That gent's tobacco juice an' lightnin'!

"And what in heck is that?"

"That's a expression what them waddies in the Florida cowcamps uses."

"Humph—first time I ever heard you'd been to Florida."

"I ain't. I got that outa a book," Pony George admitted. "There's nothin' like readin' tuh edjucate a fella's mind."

Lawler grinned faintly. "Link an' some of his cronies gave me a chase last night," he mentioned. "They quit after I dropped a couple of their broncs. Link got throwed into some prickly-pear. I expect he's feelin' a little wicked this mornin'."

"What brought that up?"

"I just seen him ridin' into town."

"Wal," grinned Pony George, "I'd sure admired tuh have seen him settin' on that cactus. Yuh wanta watch out fer that

33

pelican—he's meaner'n gar soup! I've sorta got a notion his folks, on the mother's side, wore moccasins, if yuh git what I mean. Yuh wanta keep yore eye peeled sharp.

"I'm gonna grab Link with the goods, one of these days," Lawler muttered, "an' we'll take him out of circulation. What time's it gettin' to be, George? I expect we ought to be siftin' along towards the hall. When Obe Kringle holds a inquest he sure don't hanker to have gents droppin' in late."

With a disgusted snort, Pony George glared at his watch. "The damn' thing's stopped plumb complete—an' only last week I paid that dang Jesse James jeweller five good dollars tuh make it go! Cripes, if I'd known he wasn't gonna make it go longer'n a week, I'd of saved m'five bucks an' give him the watch!"

## Chapter VII

### THE INQUEST

MUCH too near the turbulent border marked by the Rio Grande was the sleepy cow town of Pecos for the the death of a Mexican to be of any great public interest. Therefore, it was with something of surprise that Lawler and Pony George elbowed their way through the throng that overflowed the corridor outside the room set aside for the inquest on Toreva.

Seldom indeed did Obediah Kringle, the coroner, have opportunity to bask in the limelight of the public gaze. To Lawler and Pony George, as they squeezed into the tight-packed room, came the thought that Obe was determined to make the most of this occasion.

A large American flag had been tautly stretched across the dingy back wall. Before this emblem of sovereignty was placed a long bare table behind which, in solemn dignity, reposed the coroner's black-clad figure. An expression of stern righteousness, such as is sometimes worn by a new judge, sat heavily upon his unprepossessing countenance.

It seemed he was intent on surrounding the inquiry with all the pomp his vanity could suggest. As Pony George told Lawler in a loud stage whisper, "If any fool had told him he could likely use a band, he'd 'a' had all the local talent right on hand, tuh furnish noise between the witnesses remarks!"

It was rumoured that Obe *had* hinted strongly that his jury might later be treated to drinks at his expense. Anyhow, he seemed to have had scant trouble in securing the services of twelve good men and true.

Nor could he find reason, Lawler thought, to complain at the size of his prospective audience. The courtroom was jammed to the door and the corridor outside held a muttering throng.

At last Kringle arose to his awkward six-foot-four and rapped loudly on the table for attention. A secretary sat alert beside his elbow.

With the formalities finally disposed of the jury was charged that it was their bounden duty to determine, from the facts presented, whether Toreva's death was a felony, an accident, a suicide, or from natural causes. In the event that they found said death to be a felony they were to determine, if possible the identity of the guilty party.

"Your findings, gentlemen," intoned Kringle with ponderous austerity, "will be presented to the Circuit Court, together with such material evidence as may be in possession of the Sheriff's Office."

The tight-packed throng of lanky, wrinkled-faced men, belted and booted, hatted and unsmiling, overflowing the courtroom leaned forward in eager attention as Kringle handed Pony George a list of names. Expectant silence closed tight upon the perspiring assemblage.

The deputy cleared his throat. "Pony George Kasta!" he shouted, and grinned foolishly as he mounted the improvised platform of soap boxes and took the witness chair. The oath was administered in hushed solemnity.

The crowd about the doorway stirred and muttered as a burly man with tight-lipped mouth and bottle nose shoved his way inside. Lawler, seated at the coroner's table, could not suppress a start at sight of the newcomer here, although he had known the fellow was in town.

The crowd's astonishment rapidly changed to indignation.

"Link Holladay!" someone growled. "He's got a helluva nerve comin' in here!"

Holladay must have heard for his thin lips curled in a saturnine grin as he shoved a place for himself on one of the crowded benches.

Kringle rapped for silence. When the babble lulled he addressed Pony George, asking a few preliminary questions as to how long the witness had known the deceased. Having answered, the deputy was next requested to relate exactly, and in detail, the circumstances under which he had found the body.

"Wal," he drawled, having cleared his throat to insure attention, "it was like this, Obe——"

"That'll do!" snapped the coroner, red-faced. "When you've

35

got occasion to address me, have the kindness to refer to me as 'Your Honour.' "

Pony George grinned. "All right. It was like this, Obe—ah, yore honour." He paused to let the crowd snicker their appreciation. "The sheriff told me tuh keep a eye on Toreva's house las' night——"

"What for?"

"Wal, yuh see, some gent had sent him a note demandin' several thousand bucks hush money, an' Toreva wasn't aimin' tuh pay it."

"Where is this note?" demanded Kringle. "I think this is a matter of public interest. We shall have it read."

Frowning, Lawler produced the note and handed it to the coroner who, adjusting his horn-rimmed spectacles, read aloud:

"Eight thousand bucks, left to-night by the flat rock out back of yore stable, will mebbe keep yore sinful past a secret for some months longer . . . Justice."

Interest was breathless as Kringle's voice trailed off. Wiping his flushed face with a large moist handkerchief, he glared accusingly at Lawler. "Who's this Justice fella?"

"If I knew that," Lawler said, "I wouldn't be wastin' my time in here."

"Where'd the note come from?" Kringle demanded, ignoring the sheriff's sarcasm.

Pony George shrugged. "Toreva did not say."

"Then get on with your story, Kasta."

"Wal, like I was sayin' when yuh interrupted me, the sheriff gave me orders to keep m' eye out fer any suspicious gents I caught loiterin' around Toreva's house. I figgered the best way tuh do that was tuh make sure——"

"This court is not interested in what you figured. What did you *do?*"

"Huh? Wal, I set down on Toreva's front porch. With a double-barrelled shotgun in m' lap."

Pony George scowled, scratched his head, put his hat back on and resumed: "Manuel sat out there with me fer a spell. But after a while he got tired talkin' to himself an' got up. Said he was goin' inside an' I told him no one was standin' on his shirt-tail. After he went in I sat there for a right smart spell. Presently, as the fella said in the book, comin' down the street I sees that long-eared gent from over near Barstow. The fella what gives out his name is Lester. Wal, I watched him until he got off his nag an' sashayed into Miguel Garcia's cantina."

"What happened after that?" Kringle impatiently prompted.

"Nothin' happened after that. I set some more. Finally down the street comes that lunger, Joe Reede. I kep' my eye

36

on him till he got outa sight. Then I resumed m' settin'. No one else come by. Seems like everyone in town, pretty near, had gone to that carnival what's pitched its tents along the river.

"I set there chewin' fer about another hour. Then, all of a sudden-like, I hears a sorta *bump* from inside the house. Thinks I, what's that dang fool up to? Before that, yuh see, I'd heard 'im rattlin' papers an' walkin' around. But after the bumpin' sound I didn't hear nothin'. The place was quiet as the grave of Twotank-Amen. I tell yuh, it shore made me feel oneasy."

Intense interest stamped the faces of the audience. In a sort of breathless anticipation they awaited Pony George's next words.

"After a time I begun to get kind of suspicious. Anyone would not hearin' no sound. So I got up an' went inside tuh see what was up. I had told Manuel tuh leave the main room lights on, but when I got inside I found the place black as the inside of yore hat!

"I gotta admit it give me a kinda creepy feelin' in m' stomach as I felt around for that lamp. It was still hot when I found it, provin' that it hadn't been out more'n a coupla minutes. Strikin' a match I lit it. Then I looked round. The shotgun damn near dropped from m'hand!"

Pausing impressively, Pony George glanced round at the bulging eyes that watched him tensely.

"What did you see? Quit wastin' time, George," growled Kringle testily. "You ain't the only witness on this programme. Hurry up an' tell this jury what you seen."

"When I looked round I seen Toreva. He was settin' over in a corner, facin' kinda away from me an' sorta hunched-up, if yuh get what I mean. Thinks I, the darned fool's fall-en——"

"That is not the way in which to refer to the late lamented," snarled Kringle.

"Wal, yuh wanted me tuh tell 'em how I found the body, didn't yuh? Suff'rin' snakes! How can I if yuh keep buttin' in? I swore tuh tell the truth, the whole truth——"

"Go on!"

"Wal," Pony George returned the coroner's murderous glare, "mebbe yuh'd rather tell this yoreself," he growled. "Gosh knows yuh've heard it often enough tuh know 'er by heart!"

Coroner Obe Kringle almost choked, so wrath was he. "Tell your story or get off that stand!"

"Wal, I forget where—oh! I seen Toreva. He was settin' over in a corner. Thinks I, Manuel's fell asleep. 'Manu-el!'

I yells, fit tuh wake the dead. But never a peep did he make. Jest kep' a-settin' there like a bump on a log.

"Wal, I tip-toes over tuh get a better look at 'im. An' right there's where yuh coulda knocked me over with a zephyr. Gentlemen, don't talk! There was Toreva with a knife through his throat an' blood all over!"

The effect of the deputy's testimony upon the jury and the courtroom was electrical. Here, surely, said each man to his neighbour, was a sensation worthy of headlines in anybody's paper! Murder was murder—even in Pecos!

"Describe the fatal weapon, which we shall later mark 'People's exhibit A'."

"I dunno's I can," said Pony George uncomfortably. "It was jest plain everyday bone-handled skinnin' knife. But tied around its haft," he added brightly, "was a little chunk of paper."

"Indeed!" said Kringle as the crowd leaned forward expectantly. "Describe this piece of paper—better still, let me see it."

Lawler handed the smeared note to the coroner. Kringle examined it closely, passed it round among the jury, then read aloud: "Tally two for Justice."

Bewilderment stamped the faces of his listeners. He turned to Pony George. "Just what does this mean?"

"Wal, I'll tell you, Obe—last week, after that fella Doak was killed, it seems like you found a note in his pocket what said somethin' about the climate here not bein' over-healthy for the fishermen of Toyah Lake. That note, like this 'un, yuh remember, was signed by that fella 'Justice.' It's the opinion of the Sheriff's office that this fella killed both Doak an' Toreva."

Excitement claimed the courtroom. Kringle rapped for order. "You may step down from the stand, George. Call the next witness."

"What's the use? Yuh got yore——"

"Call the next witness!"

"Doctor Obediah Kringle, sawbones an' coroner, will now be right pleased tuh take the stand," grunted Pony George and, grinning, slid his chunky form into a chair beside the sheriff.

"Cut out the funny stuff, George," growled Lawler in an undertone. "This ain't the place or occasion for such antics."

With great solemnity Kringle mounted the soap box platform, administered and took the oath, perched himself gingerly upon the extreme edge of the witness chair and surveyed the jury gravely.

"What's he figgerin' tuh do?" asked the irrepressible deputy. "Gonna give 'em a blessin' or bawl 'em out?"

A snicker ran through the nearby spectators. Kringle flushed. "Silence, there, or I'll clear this room!" Then in a graveyard voice he announced:

"Having performed an autopsy on the body of the late deceased, I found him to have a fractured parietal bone and a penetrating stab wound in the neck. The latter was undoubtedly the cause of death."

Lawler, interested, put a question. "Was the fracture sustained recently?"

"Yes. Within one minute of his death."

"You mean some gent struck him before he was stabbed?"

"It is my theory that someone struck him, yes. With a blunt and, evidently, pliable instrument."

"No sign of the skin havin' been broken?"

"Certainly not. There was a bruise—nothing more."

"Would you say the bruise an' fracture could have been caused by a blackjack?"

"Not only could have been, but was. I," Kringle's voice ill-suppressed the sense of triumph which he felt, "have the weapon in my possession."

To say that Lawler was startled would be to understate the truth. He was amazed. He looked accusingly at Pony George. George licked his lips and focused his incredulous glance upon the coroner who was relinquishing the witness chair.

"Say that again!" growled Pony George.

"I said that the blackjack's in my possession."

"Where'd yuh get it?"

"Well," Kringle paused, "I was not satisfied with what you had originally told me about finding Toreva. I thought," he said mockingly, "that it was quite possible you might have overlooked some pertinent bit of evidence in searching Toreva's house after finding the body. I was confirmed in my suspicions—"

Pony George jumped to his feet. "Yore *what!*" he snarled.

"Well, perhaps I should have said 'my convictions,'" amended Kringle. "I was confirmed in my convictions when I found, during the autopsy, that Toreva had recently sustained a fracture of the parietal bone. So I went over the house thoroughly, after persauding the old woman who took care of the place that I was not going to steal anything."

"When was this?" asked Lawler.

"Early this morning. *I*," his chest expanded pridefully, "went over the room carefully. I found the blackjack by a rear window where it had evidently fallen from the killer's pocket as he made his getaway."

39

"I'd like to have it produced in evidence." Lawler's tone was grim.

"We will mark it 'Exhibit B,'" smiled Kringle broadly. Thrusting a hand inside his coat he produced the blackjack and passed it around among the jurors. The faces of those who examined it seemed to freeze.

"Mr. Foreman of the Jury," spoke Kringle suavely, "will you be so kind as to read the words burned into the leather of exhibit B?"

The foreman rose. Clearing his throat several times as though nervous, he announced, "The name on this thing is 'Link Holladay.'"

·The sudden hush that gripped the room was broken by a curse as Holladay surged to his feet. "So that's why yuh sent for me to be here, is it? You damn sidewinder! That's a lie! I never owned a blackjack in my life!"

"The foreman licked his lips uneasily. He shrank back among his fellows.

"A lie?" mocked Kringle. "Well, I only know that your name is burned ot it. Seems odd anyone else would put your name on their property. Here, you can look for yourself——"

"Oh, no, he can't," snapped Lawler quickly. "I'll take charge of that blackjack, Kringle. Hand it here."

As the coroner passed it over Holladay snarled:

"By Gawd, it's a dirty frame-up! You can't hang this murder on me, Lawler! You know damn well I wasn't in town! You saw me——"

"Yeah. I saw you, all right. But there was nothin' to keep you from ridin' to town an' murderin' Toreva after I left you."

"You know I didn't have no hoss——"

"Some of your friends had horses," Lawler pointed out. "I'm afraid, my friend, I shall be compelled to place you under lock an' key——"

"Like hell you will!" Holladay's hand dived for his hip where swung the butt of a holstered .45—though it was a violation of the law to carry arms inside town limits. But Holladay's hand never reached his gun. Men grabbed at him from all sides, pinioned his arms and legs and held him fast. His face was a twisted snarl as he cursed them with lurid fury.

After Holladay had been escorted to the jail, disarmed and placed in a cell (charged, for convenience, with unlawfully carrying weapons), the inquest upon the violent death of Manuel Toreva was continued.

Lester, the man who had drifted into the country and had

40

built a shack near Barstow and who had a strange habit of spending most of his time in Pecos, was the last witness called to the stand.

Lester, big-eared, tall and powerfully-built, with smouldering dark eyes in a high-boned face, was sworn in swiftly. After the preliminary questions, Kringle asked:

"Mr. Lester, will you kindly explain to the gentlemen of this jury what you saw last night as you were about to leave this town for home?"

"Sure," grinned Lester. "I had jest left Garcia's cantina an' was forkin' my bronc down the street back of Toreva's place, sorta figgerin' mebbe I'd oughta head for home, when I seen a fella slip through Toreva's back gate an' climb aboard a hoss that was standin' on grounded reins."

"Mr. Lester, I'd like to have you tell us what in your estimation, that man was."

"Wal, it was pretty dark, yuh understand. It had been tolerable cloudy all evenin'—probably rained someplace, I guess. Anyhow, it was considerable dark an' so I ain't right sure, not gettin' a look at the fella's pan. But I think the gent what came through Toreva's back gate was that Holladay jasper which yuh jest lugged off to jail."

After the buzz of excitement had somewhat abated, Kringle asked: "How do you make that out. I mean, if it was dark and you couldn't see his face what makes you think it was Holladay?"

"I could see he was a big hombre, heavy-set an' all. I dunno, but I sorta got the impression that it was Holladay somehow. When he seen me, he climbed aboard his bronc an' made dust. I got sorta suspicious then. Instead of goin' home, I got myself a room at the Orient an' stayed over."

"Did you know that murder had been commited?"

"Nope. I didn't know as anythin' had been com—well, whatever yuh called it. I expect I was jest curious. That fella lit out in such a hurry . . ."

"All right, you may leave the stand." Kringle shot a glance at the jury. "Do any of you gents want to ask questions of any of the witnesses?"

The jury shook their heads.

"Very well, then, gentlemen," Kringle removed his spectacles, carefully wiped their lenses and returned them to his nose. "We've heard a number of interesting things this morning and, ah—by the way, Sheriff. I think the jury had better be shown the fatal weapon. I am referring to the knife with which Manuel Toreva was murdered."

Lawler frowned. "I'm sorry, Kringle, but I can't oblige. Pony George locked the knife in my desk last night. But someone broke the lock and well, the thing has vanished."

41

"What is this you're trying to tell me?"

"The knife," said Lawler grimly, "is gone."

It was several noisy moments before the coroner could make himself heard. "Silence!" he hammered furiously on the table. "Shut up, damn it!"

And when the crowd had quieted——

"That's criminal negligence——"

But Lawler stopped him. "I've heard all I care to on the subject. I'm accountable for the knife—not you. Get on with your talk."

Ironing out his scowl, Kringle again faced the jury. "We have heard some interesting things this morning, gentlemen. Some *very* interesting things," he added nastily. "There is no use in dragging this inquest along further. Every important bit of information in our possession has been divulged. You may withdraw to determine your verdict——"

"Not necessary," muttered the foreman, and cleared his throat. With a glance at his fellow jurymen, he said nervously:

"We bring in a verdict of murder at the hands of some person, or persons, unknown—but we think it was committed by the fella what signs himself 'Justice.' "

## Chapter VIII

### "MURDER'S NEVER OUTLAWED!"

LAWLER and his deputy left the courtroom with the stream of shoving, pushing, grunting men flowing from its opened door at the close of Kringle's inquest. Being close to the noon hour, at which time Pony George had become accustomed to "feeding his face," the chunky deputy could not restrain a number of longing glances from straying in the direction of a sign which read: Lone Star Grub Emporium. Glances, it might be added, which Lawler pointedly ignored.

"Kringle run a fast one on us," the sheriff said coldly, "when he produced that blackjack in evidence."

"Cripes! These amateurs!" Pony George growled. "I don't know anything which gives me a bigger pain."

"When amateurs discover more than a paid professional, it's high time prof grabbed a hold on himself." Lawler's tones grew colder with every sentence uttered.

Pony George shot him a covert glance. In the sheriff's eye he detected a glint that was hinting large toward imminent trouble. He tugged his drooping yellow moustache nervously.

"Suff'rin' snakes!" he grumbled. "All yuh tol' me tuh do was tuh keep a eye on Toreva's house. I done 'er. Then findin' him dead with a knife in his crop it never struck me that I'd ort tuh gone over the carpet with a magnifyin' glass an' a fine-tooth comb! Nor I didn't figger I was supposed tuh pore plaster all over the place takin' casts of imaginary footprints like them Hollywood jaspers do in all their cock-eyed pitchers! Hell's bells—I ain't no Spurlock Holmes!"

"You sure told the truth that time," Lawler retorted drily.

"Wal, good sakes! How'd I know the fool Mex went an' got his prital bone cracked? Hell, I never knowed a Mex had that kinduva bone! What kinda thing is it, anyway?"

"It's a bone in the side of most people's heads. But that ain't what I'm referrin' to. You oughta been able to spot that blackjack."

"That's right—rub it in, rub it in! By cripes, I got a notion tuh kick that dang coroner halfway tuh El Paso! Why can't he mind his own business? It sure is boomin' these days!"

Hands thrust deep within his pockets, Red Lawler was standing inattentive by his desk, his brooding eyes fixed unseeingly upon the broken lock of the pilfered drawer.

"Funny about Holladay showin' up. Wonder if Kringle *did* send for him? Can't see how he'd get hold of him. Link's strong on driftin' . . ." Musingly Lawler added. " 'Death by person, or persons, unknown . . .' "

Pony George growled, "Yeah—the bunch of ol' women! They was scared plumb stiff of Link. Any fool could see it. They'd no more thought of accusin' him of that murder than of slashin' their own throats!"

"I expect they did right. I ain't at all sure Link's our man. No doubt about him twirlin' a wide loop, though. I'll be gettin' him for that, one of these days. But murder——"

"Wal," Pony George chipped in, "he shore gave you one murderous look when yuh told him yuh was goin' to slap 'im in jail!"

"But if Link was innocent, you can't hardly blame him for bein' a bit proddy."

"Yeah," said Pony George with fine sarcasm. "*If* he's innocent!"

"Well, let's take a look at him."

When Lawler and his deputy were seen by Link Holladay to be standing outside the door to his cell, the rustler's thin lips twisted into an ugly sneer.

"You fellas got yore cinches crossed," he jeered. "This

43

ain't visitin' day at the zoo. I'll thank yuh to get the hell outa here an' leave me a little privacy."

"Why, Link!" Pony George said reprovingly. "We was figgerin' tuh bring yuh some posies an' a book of psalms—rest an' meditation bein' good fer the soul."

When Pony George had gone the sheriff sat listlessly watching a large horse-fly washing its face in the sweat beading the water-cooler's exterior.

"You ain't funny," snarled Holladay, scowling. "An' I'll take pleasure in wipin' that grin off yore homely mug soon's I get outa here."

"I don't know's yuh're goin' to get out, Link. It all depends——"

"Yes," said Lawler. "Suppose you open up an' treat us to a heart-to-heart talk."

"I got nothin' tuh say," Holladay growled. "You know as well as I do, Red Lawler, that I didn't stab that greaser. You an' me was exchangin' rifle shots out on the range last night."

"That's so. But it is barely possible that you beat me to town. An' if you did, I reckon you had time enough to murder poor Manuel an' make your getaway by that back gate . . ."

"What the hell you talkin' about? I don't know nothin' about no back gate, an' you can't make out I do."

"We don't have tuh make it out," chuckled Pony George. "That big-eared gent from Barstow done that after we dragged you off tuh jail. Lester said he saw you comin' out Toreva's back gate. An' the time checks up slick as a whistle."

"It's a damn frame-up!" bellowed Holladay. "I never done it!" His ugly chin shot forward belligerently, "When I get outa here I'm shore gonna make somebody hard tuh catch!"

"Then I reckon we'll keep you right where you are, for a spell," said Lawler, softly. "I don't see no sense in takin' unnecessary chances with gents of your antecedents. You're a tough egg, Link, an' this rest will do you good."

Back in the Sheriff's office, Pony George said:

"That fella's bad medicine, Red. If we let him loose another murder would foller sure as summer follers spring!"

"There's one thing sure," he muttered morosely. "If I let Holladay loose a couple gents are goin' to find themselves up against a Texas cyclone—an' I don't mean me an' Pony George!"

Presently his thoughts turned as ever to Sara Tranton. What lay behind her incomprehensible action in breaking off their engagement? The whole business seemed alien to her nature as he knew it. At first he had been too hurt and angry to think clearly on the subject. But now that his red-headed nature had had time to cool, he found himself unable to believe she no longer cared for him.

"I'll be jiggered if *I* can figure it out!" he exclaimed. "It's sure got me fightin' my hat!"

The most logical explanation he could think of was that Sara had told her father of their engagement and he, disapproving, had bidden her break it off. But why? He and the Captain had always got along handsomely.

Yet, good as he knew Dan Tranton to be to his only daughter, it did not seem like her to throw down the man she loved simply to please his idle whim of selfish desire to keep her to himself.

In the language of the West Texas cow country, Sara Tranton was a girl of backbone. She had, as Red well knew, qualities of grit and loyalty far beyond the ordinary. Too, she had a bulldog tenacity—if she loved a man, he thought, she'd stick to him come hell or high-water.

The least she could have done would have been to tell him fairly that her father disapproved and to have suggested that they wait until somehow they should win him to their side.

But no! She had termed their engagement "Silly!"

With a baffled snort Red Lawler temporarily gave up trying to solve the problem of her strange behaviour. He could discern neither head nor tail to the puzzle, and felt that if he wrestled longer with it in his present mood he would surely do something downright desperate.

A clump of boots and the jingle of dragging spur chains announced the return of Pony George. Entering the office, the chunky deputy tossed his hat on the Sheriff's desk. Drawing up a chair beside the water-cooler, he terminated the fastidious ablutions of the large horse-fly bathing languorously upon its sweat-beaded surface.

"Hotter'n election day in a hornet's nest," he growled, mopping his face with his neckerchief. "Red, this here's the thirstiest country I ever seen."

"I expect you ain't never been to Gila Bend," said Lawler, grinning. "Nor Yuma. Nor yet Needles. Ah, Needles—there's a hot place for you. It's got hell backed off the map. Averages round about a hundred an' thirty-six in the daytime an' at night she sweats you down like a tallow candle. Folks livin' there does all their cookin' out in the sand of their front door-yards. An' has to feed their chickens cracked ice to keep 'em from layin' hard-boiled eggs!"

Pony George sniffed. "Yeah? Wal, Pecos has got all the heat *I* ever wanta see. An' I don't like aiggs nohow. Speakin' of aiggs, Red, reminds me of a new verse I've writ—

"The rest o' the gals thet danced in the Flame,

45

Was ornery, too, I opine——
But the boys from the range that haunted the town,
Came mostly with Lou fer to jine.

"An' gosh, thet gives me a idee for another! Listen at this, fella:

"Now Cal was right jealous—By Gawd, but he was!
An' he wanted young Lou fer his own;
So he warned off the boys thet came in from the range,
An' he put ev'ry meddler 'neath stone!

"Gosh—ain't that a pistol!"

"Couldn't say. I'm not an authority on firearms."

"Wal, for the love of Mike! Who's talkin' about firearms? I ast yuh ain't that highferlootin' poetry."

"Oh—the poetry. Is that what it was?" Lawler, about to duck the paperweight Pony George was reaching for, suddenly tensed. "Shh!"

The corridor outside rang to the clump of spurred boots. Lawler shot a hurried glance through the window. "Strange horse outside. Reckon we're gettin' company."

There was one stranger in the county whom neither the sheriff or his deputy had yet seen. There was good reason for the fact; this stranger was something of a recluse, was admittedly shy of strange faces and did most of his travelling by night. Furthermore, so far he had been steering a careful course that avoided the county seat.

He was a little man with sharp eyes that glanced uneasily from face to face. His bat-wing chaps had seen much wear, his cotton shirt was dusty and patched in many places. His hat was a thing too disreputable to attract more than a passing glance from a range tramp. He entered the office with a sidling motion and when he paused before Lawler's desk, stood shuffling his feet nervously.

"Restless as a wet hen," Pony George commented *sotto voce*.

"This the sheriff's office?" the stranger's voice was a husky squeak.

"Nope," Pony George spoke promptly. "This here's the headquarters for the Knights of Rest. Light down, comrade, an' rest yore saddle. Gotcha dues paid up?"

The dusty stranger blinked, looked suspiciously from Pony George to the sheriff, whose star was plain to be seen. "I—I thought," he began hesitantly, when Pony George interrupted with—

" 'Tain't noways necessary in this lodge, pardner. The Supreme Sea-Gull takes care o' that."

46

"What's on your mind, stranger?" Lawler cut short his deputy's fun.

"Why—er—nothin' much, I reckon," the man essayed a nervous smile. "Uh—I wonder could you gents tell a driftin' pilgrim how to get to Dan Tranton's place? I—I'm kinda strange to this part of the country."

"An' how!" agreed Pony George. "I never seen anythin' like yuh in all my borned days! Where'd yuh hail from?"

"Why, er—ah—I jest sort of drifted over from east of here."

"That's coverin' a heap of territory, pilgrim," Pony George eyed the little stranger suspiciously. "I reckon yuh better keep on driftin'. They tell me the climate's somethin' elegant over in Mexico. Ever been there? . . . Wal, I suggest yuh try 'er out."

"But—uh—you see, I'd sort of like to visit a spell with Tranton. Him an' me's ol' buddies. We've et from the same tin plate. Ain't his spread called the Box Bar T?"

Lawler, looking the stranger over, had a feeling that the peculiar pale blue of his eyes might be common to great strategists and notorious killers. "Yes," he answered, "Tranton runs the Box Bar T. You say you know the Captain?"

"Uh—I believe I used to know him," the stranger cautiously replied.

Lawler exchanged swift glances with Pony George. There was something about this self-confessed drifter.

"S'pose yuh describe this here Tranton fer us," Pony George suggested.

The stranger shifted his pale eyes uneasily. "Why, he's a sort of tall, rangy, black-haired gent——"

"I expect," drawled Lawler, cutting in, "you've got the wrong Tranton. Captain Dan's a white-headed gent an' averages some considerable round 'the waist."

"It might be him. I ain't seen him in fourteen-fifteen years. I been figurin' mebbe he'd give me some kind of a ridin' job. How do I get out there?"

"Not so fast, fella," Lawler said. "There's been a powerful lot too many strangers floatin' round this county durin' the last coupla months. From now on I'm aimin' to look up their pedigrees before I put out the welcome mat. What did you say your name was?"

"I didn't say," grinned the man ingratiatingly. "But it's Smith."

"Smith what?"

"Smith's the last name. First name's Max."

"Max Smith, eh? Do you know anyone else round this neck of the timber?"

"Friend of mine named Doak drifted over this way a spell back . . ."

"Well you can cross him off your callin' list. His mark's been taken off the board."

"Yuh mean to say he's—he's dead?"

"That's right. He was rubbed out a couple weeks ago. Know anyone else?"

The stranger swallowed in what seemed to be a painful manner, ran a dirty finger round the inside of his dirty collar. "I know a fella what runs a place known as the Raego spread —gent named Joe Reede. Calls his place the Lazy R, I heard."

"You heard right," Lawler said, and thrust out his hand. "Your connection's sound, Smith. I'm glad to meet up with you. My name's Lawler—I'm sheriff. This here's my deputy, Pony George Kasta."

"Glad tuh make you gents' acquaintance," said Smith shaking hands.

Lawler did not like the nervous grin on this stranger's face, but he kept the fact to himself. "You get to the Box Bar T," he directed, "by followin' that trail down there—see? The one goin' over that ridge yonder," Lawler pointed out the window and the stranger bobbed his head.

A moment later, with hurried thanks, the man calling himself Max Smith took his departure.

Soon as he was out of the door Pony George jumped from his chair, spun the combination of the sheriff's safe and swung open its thick steel door. Reaching in he dragged forth a great pile of miscellaneous papers, yellow, tattered with age— reward notices.

Lawler grinned knowingly as Pony George pawed through the dusty pile. "I expect you noticed Smith's left hand. Unusual to see a gent with the index finger missin'. Probably don't mean anything, though."

"The heck it don't," growled Pony George with fine disregard for grammar. "Three fingers an' a thumb on the left hand—I seen a notice in this bunch a while back that read almost word for word like that."

"So you been lookin' through those flyers, have you? Gettin' uncommon industrious. How far back they go?"

"Far enough. There's references to the Toyah Lake bunch, But no pitchers. I reckon them birds wasn't what yuh'd call 'partial' tuh havin' their mugs plastered round the country. Stage an' bank robbin's *one* perfession what can't see any advantage in advertisin'."

Lawler nodded. "When you find that stuff, put it where we can get our hands on it real quick. No tellin' when we may be needin' it."

Pony George gave him a curious look. "Where you goin'?"

"Right now I'm goin' to grab a bite to eat—if there's anything left. If I ain't back here in a reasonable amount of time, you can figure I've gone out to Box Bar T. I'm admittin' to a little curiosity about that Smith jigger. If Captain Dan knows him that'll mean one thing, mebbe. If he don't, it'll mebbe mean somethin' else again."

"Can't yuh talk American?" Pony George complained.

Lawler grinned. "It's just possible," he said, "that this Smith hombre is the gent that took those shots at Dan last night."

"You puttin' on?"

Lawler's grin grew broader. But he did not answer his deputy's question. Instead he said, "My stomach's tellin' me to get a move on. Crimes like stage an' bank robbery make interestin' study for earnest deputies. George, so you keep right on lookin' up them things. Not that they're apt to do us any great amount of good. Such crimes are forgiven after a period of years—'outlawed' is the term."

"Yeah?" grunted Pony George. "Well, murder's never outlawed! An' the paper I'm lookin' for is headed 'Murder!' "

## Chapter IX

### CONCERNING SMITH

WHEN Lawler left the office the deputy dropped his stack of musty papers and clumped to the door. For some while he stood there peering out. He watched the sheriff stride down the street and enter the stable where he kept his horse. A few moments later he saw Lawler emerge atop his big roan gelding.

Lawler was a good horseman and sat the saddle with an easy grace. His big shoulders seemed to slouch a little forward and there was, the deputy thought, an unaccustomed bleakness to face.

For some moments after Lawler had swung his mount into the trail leading to the Box Bar T, Pony George stood watching by the doorway. Shoving back his hat to scratch his head, he muttered, "Plumb forgot tuh eat his dinner first. Must be right anxious tuh get out there."

Finally he returned to his task, but the lackadaisical manner in which he thumbed through the faded notices proved that his mind was not on the work. When, eventually, he found the flyers for which he had been searching, he hardly glanced at them. Thrusting them carelessly into his shirt pocket, he got out his pad of paper, his stub of pencil and prepared to engage in the serious and competitive business of manufacturing poetry.

But preparation and actual achievement, he had often found, were two decidely different things. There had been occasions, he recalled, when he had sat for hours, pencil in hand and pad on knee, without the production of a single word. The present bade fair to be such an occasion.

He wet the pencil on his tongue, screwed his dried-apple countenance into one vast array of deep-etched wrinkles, and wet the pencil-point again. But all to no avail. The pad's top sheet remained a virgin white.

Suddenly, then, with neither preliminary tremor nor other warning, the pencil raced across the pad, leaving in its wake a series of ungainly scrawls resembling hen tracks which—when deciphered—would have formed a string of words in this rotation:

"One night at the Flame, Cal an' his dame  
Was havin' a damn mean row———"

It was many minutes before Pony George, licking his pencil frequently, was able to add:

"When in through the door stepped a tall slim gent,  
With his hat pulled low on his brow."

The large horse-fly was again at its ablutions on the water-cooler. Cocking an eye in its direction, Pony George said in a voice that was tremulous:

"Gosh! Ain't that a corker!"

But the horse-fly only buzzed away.

It was five o'clock that afternoon when, going to the door at the sound of approaching hoofbeats, the manufacturing poet saw Lawler riding up the street leading an extra horse. Stuffing pencil and pad hurriedly into his hip pocket, Pony George ran a knarled hand over his drooping straw-coloured moustache and muttered:

"Sure looks like Red wa'n't ast tuh stay an' eat."

As his young boss drew closer the puckered eyes in George's dried-apple face drew wide with startled interest. When Lawler swung from the big roan gelding and tethered both horses to the rack before the courthouse the chunky deputy remained, still staring, in the doorway.

Mounting the steps Lawler pushed him protesting down

the corridor and into the office. Outside the sun still shone bright and the air was hot and dust-filled, yet Lawler insisted on closing the door.

"Did you locate them notices, George?"

"Sure— 'course I did," Pony George pulled the papers from his shirt and thrust them out. There were three, and Lawler read them with a scowl. They were all alike:

## WANTED FOR MURDER

### $3,000——Dead or alive

Max Smith, alias Four-Finger Durr. Five feet two. Weighs about 120 pounds. Brown hair and small blue eyes. Smooth-shaven usually. Eyes shifty. Has old bullet wound in right shoulder, another in left thigh. Occupation, cowhand. Uses one gun——*fast*. Carries .30-.30 rifle in saddle scabbard. Has shy, nervous manner but will fight if cornered. Known to be a member of Toyah Lake gang. Officers warned to be careful. Durr has missing index finger on left hand.

"That's the fella," he said, as he finished reading.

"Where'd yuh get his hoss, Red?"

"You know the trail that goes out past the Box Bar T? You remember that little tree-clad hill with the junipers 'bout four miles from Captain Dan's—the place where Link an' me exchanged shots last night? . . . Well, right along this side the hill I found Durr's horse standin' tied to a cactus."

"Didn't get tuh go tuh Tranton's then? Did yuh find Durr's body?"

"What give you the idea it was there to be found?"

"Wal, I jest sort of opined it was by the look on yore face. Did yuh find it?"

"Yeah—beside the horse. He was sprawled on the trail, face down."

"Dead, eh?"

"Yeah. Dead. There was a bullet hole between his eyes an' powder marks on his face. He must been in the saddle talkin' with the killer, not thinkin' to be bumped off. No sign of a struggle. Killer must have drew an' fired while Durr was palaverin'. I seen the tracks of the killer's horse."

"Foller 'em?"

"Naturally. Followed 'em far's I could—which wasn't far. Lost 'em in a maze of other tracks 'bout a mile from town. Unless he's done some tall an' handsome circlin', that killer's in Pecos right this minute. Prob'ly laughin' up his sleeve."

Pony George, well aware of Lawler's repute as a trailer of no mean skill, looked the astonishment he felt. More than once it had been said that Lawler was one gent who could follow a trail to hell, and back. He had often been likened to a wolfhound; keen, tireless, unshakable as Death itself.

Yet George had just listened to him admit that this mysterious killer had eluded him, had gotten clean away. Small wonder Pony George pursed his lips in a soundless whistle. "Where's the body?"

"I packed it back to town an' left it with Kringle."

"Must be gettin' plumb absent-minded," growled the deputy. "Yuh forgettin' thet blackjack episode? Hell! that fella's apt tuh perduce Durr's pedigree by starin' at his fingernails, an' haul his paw outa Durr's hat with a fistful of loot from the Toyah Lake days!"

"Not hardly. I've been through Durr's clothes pretty careful. This here," said Lawler softly, flicking a scrap of yellow paper across the desk, "was buttoned on his shirt. We won't tell Kringle."

Gingerly Pony George picked up the paper and spread it out. "Three down—some more to go!" This note, like the ones preceding it, was signed "Justice."

"Reckon he figgered 'twould be a good idee tuh keep Durr away from Cap'n Dan. But I can't see why less'n he thought Durr might have somethin' tuh spill an' be aimin' tuh do so."

"I got no idea what he thought," Lawler admitted. "Far as I'm concerned, the whole affair's a complete muddle. Fact is, George, I ain't even sure Durr was goin' to the Box Bar T."

"Wal, cripes! He was on his way, wa'n't he?"

Lawler's voice was grim. "That don't signify."

"But sufferin' snakes—all that talk! He *said* he was goin' out there. Said him an' the Cap'n was ol' bunkies, or somethin' tuh that effect."

"Smoke screen," Lawler opined, succinctly. "Camouflage —hot air."

"Wal then, he sure went to a powerful lot o' trouble, that's all I gotta say."

"Of course," Lawler admitted, "Durr *may* actually have been headin' for Tranton's."

"But yuh jest said——"

"Skip it! I ain't in no mood to argue, George. My head aches like a trip-hammer."

"Wal, if he *was* goin' out there tuh see the Cap'n, do yuh reckon mebbe he was thinkin' of blackmail?"

"It's possible. If Durr really knew the bunch he claimed he knew, it might be said to indicate that all of 'em had once belonged to the Toyah Lake outfit. I think, however, it might mean a lot of other things. Durr may have been lyin'. Durr

52

may have known one of those gents. If so, does it seem logical he would let it be known he was aimin' to visit him?"

"Wal, good gosh! After all that gassin' I'm damned if I know what we was palaverin' about in the first place!" Pony George growled disgustedly. "Let's change the subject—wanta hear my latest verse?"

"What are you talkin' about?"

"My ballad of Kyote Cal. M' latest verse is a honey. Wanta hear it?"

"No—I got too many other things to think about right now. By the way, where'd you borrow the tune?"

"Borry? Why, hell! I made it up. Do yuh like it?"

" 'Bout as well as I like the words, I guess."

Pony George sniffed. "Trouble is with you, yuh ain't got no ear for music."

"I can hear *music*, all right," Lawler said, and switched the subject. "Look who's comin' up the walk. That Reede gent. Now let me do the talkin', George. I think this bird's smelled trouble."

## *Chapter X*

### "HE'S GONNA KILL US ALL!"

BOTH lawmen turned toward the door as booted feet came clumping down the corridor. Abruptly the door flung open.

"My, my, my!" clucked Pony George. "Ain't yuh never learned tuh knock?"

A tall gangling man in wrinkled black clothes that hung to his bony frame like the cast-off garments of a scarecrow stood in the open doorway. He turned a wrinkled face to Pony George—a face that was chalky white in a land where men were bronzed.

"Howdy, Deputy. How you feelin'?"

"Finer'n a hummin-bird's pin-feathers! How's yoreself?"

"I have been better," Reede admitted. He turned to Lawler. "That right what I heard about some stranger gettin' rubbed out?"

"What did you hear?"

"I heard some fella got snuffed out over near Tranton's. That right?" And at the sheriff's nod, "Looks kinda bad for Tranton, I'd say."

"Does it?" Lawler eyed the consumptive coldly. "I don't expect I'd go so far as to say that. To my mind it looks much worse for a couple other gents I could name. Guess you been talkin' to them bar-room loafers that saw me packin' the stranger in. By the way, Reede," he added as an apparent afterthought, "gent gave his name as Smith—Max Smith. Stopped in here a while this noon. Said he was a friend of yours."

Reede shrugged and took the seat by the water-cooler. "Lotsa gents claim they're friends of mine. I can't think of any Smith. What sort of a lookin' jasper was he?"

Lawler's eyes were inscrutable as he leaned forward on his desk and stared at Reede. Then casually he took some papers from his pocket, glanced at them and said, "Well, Max Smith was five feet two, weighed one-twenty, he had light brown hair an' pale, shifty blue eyes. He was togged out in things so run down a range tramp woulda blushed to be seen dead in." Looking up, Lawler's jade-green glance beat hard against Reede's face.

Reede said, "I don't recognize that description. Is it official?"

"Had any experience with such things?"

Reede's lips twisted in a cold smile. "Hell, a man don't need experience to know a reward notice when he sees it! So Smith was a bad 'un, eh?"

"I'm thinkin' you knew him better'n me. What did you think of him?"

But Reede only smiled. "I never met the gent. By the way," he broke off with a hacking cough that shook his bony form from heels to head. When the paroxysm passed he wiped his colourless lips. "I hear ol' Cap'n Dan was shot at in his office las' night."

"For a man who don't get around much, you certainly hear a lot. Where'd you get that information?"

Reede grinned and a cold glitter came into his eyes like sun on windswept ice. "A little bird whispered it in my ear."

"By G——" Lawler broke off as the telephone rang. Scooping up the receiver he growled, "Sheriff Lawler speaking . . . Oh! Long Distance, eh? All right, put 'em on! . . . Huh? Who? . . . Lester? . . . When? . . . Okay, Ed. Keep your eyes skinned."

"What's up?" demanded Pony George when Lawler faced them. "Quit lookin' like yo' in a trance an'——" he paused as Lawler grabbed a sheet of paper and hastily began scribbling.

Looking up, Lawler made a visible effort to pull himself together. "Hustle this down to the telegraph office," he said, handing the paper to Pony George, "an' see that it gets off right away. Tell the operator to bring the answer here. If I ain't here, tell him to leave it on my desk. Now step on it! I'll tell you about that phone call soon's you get back."

Lawler's face was nearly pale as that of Reede! About his mouth were new, pinched lines. In his eyes was a strangely troubled light. Moisture glistened on his upper lip and forehead.

Pony George, for once, did not stop to argue. As he left there was a tiny sharp burst of sound outside the open window —such a sound as might be made by a snapping twig beneath a booted foot.

Lawler sprang to the window, startled. But though he thrust his head and shoulders out he saw nothing unusual. No man was in sight nor did hear any sound that resembled a hurried retreat.

"Reckon I'm developin' a case of nerves," he grunted, pulling in his head.

Reede did not smile. He stared at Lawler straightly; appraisingly, one might have said. Eyes jade-green and eyes of faded blue locked and neither pair wavered. It was like a duel.

On a shelf a battered clock ticked off the dragging minutes. Presently Pony George returned, dropped perspiring into the chair behind the desk; the chair Lawler had vacated. "Wal," he puffed, "let's hear about that long-distance phone call. I been fair a-quiver with curiosity."

"From Ed Lamb, at Barstow," Lawler said. "Big-Ear Lester was just found dead outside his shack—been dead for several hours, Ed says. He'd been stabbed in the back an' had one of them 'Justice' notes in his chaps pocket."

"Big—Ear—Lester!" the whispered words crept through the twisted lips of Reede's livid face. Abruptly, then, an hysterical laugh spread wide his mouth and showed his pointed teeth. "Lester!" he echoed. "Doak—Tranton—Durr—*Lester!* Why the crazy coot's gone batty! He's tryin' to kill us all!" and, with a final snarling oath, he lunged from the office, broke into a headlong run when he hit the street.

Lawler stared at Pony George. Pony George stared back.

## Chapter XI

### KRINGLE SHOWS HIS TEETH

"DAFFY as a gopher!" said Pony George with conviction.

"I ain't so sure about that. There's somethin'——"
Leaving the sentence unfinished, Lawler began to pace the office with hands deep-thrust in his pockets, shoulders hunched

a little forward and a fierce look of determined concentration in his brooding eyes.

"If he ain't plumb batty," sniffed Pony George, getting out his pipe, "then he's sure doin' one powerful lot of puttin' on." He tinkered with his pipe for a number of moments in the hope that Lawler would toss over his sack of Durham. But Lawler was too enwrapped in his thoughts. With a grunt the deputy pulled out his own.

Then Lawler spoke. "I've been thinkin' that mebbe Big-Ear Lester was this 'Justice' fella. Now Reede's gone and smashed that theory plumb to splinders. 'He's tryin' to kill us all!' Them's the words he used. An' Lester's killed already so that leaves him out of our future calculations."

"So what?" growled Pony George. "Jest bein' dead don't prove he ain't the Pecos Killer. One of his perspective victims —providin' there's any left—mighta got wise an' beat him to the bump. Don't that sound?"

"It sounds," admitted Lawler, "but it's off-key, George. Reede's words rule it out as a possibility. He said: *'The crazy coot's gone batty! He's trying to kill us all!'* "

"Talk—an' talk's cheaper'n flies at brandin' time."

"Ah!" said Lawler softly.

"What yuh mean by that?"

"Well, look here. This killer's nobody's fool. He's slick, cunning, ruthless. He's a man who knows what he's after an' is aimin' to get it. He's not figurin' to let anyone stand in his way. He's got some reason, I'd say, to do away with Doak, Toreva, Durr an' Big-Ear Lester. There's a connection between them fellas someplace. We know he tried to polish off Captain Dan. It's my opinion he'll try again."

"Can't see why he'd be so dang anxious tuh plant these gents," Pony George objected. "What's he got on 'em, or or them on him?"

"Must be somethin' behind it."

"Then he's keepin' it dang well hidden."

"That's open to doubt. The men who are being killed must represent a very real danger or the killer wouldn't be riskin' his neck to get 'em out of the way."

He resumed his pacing, a thoughtful expression in his vacant glance. "At least we know that Smith was once the Durr of the Toyah Lake bunch. Seems to me each of the killers other victims might likewise once have been a member of that gang."

"Don't look at me," grunted Pony George. "I can't make head nor tail——"

"It's possible," Lawler broke in, "that the killer was once a victim of some outrage of the gang, and has at last tracked

56

the surviving members down with the idea of exacting vengeance."

"Don't sound a heap likely tuh me," Pony George growled, puffing on his pipe. "Like I said before, I ain't no Spurlock Holmes, but it don't look like tuh me no fella would be apt tuh nurse such burnin' hate for a period of fifteen years. Bird like Link Holladay might. Still, I wouldn't bet on it."

"Holladay? Guess you're barkin' up the wrong tree, there. Link's been under lock an' key too long to have been the killer of Lester. An' it's my notion these murders are all the work of the same dry-gulchin' polecat. 'Tain't sensible to think we got more'n one killer slappin' leather here in Pecos."

"Humph! 'Tain't sensible to figger we got any, if it comes tuh that."

Lawler paused beside his desk. "Here's another angle. Why should this hombre sign his murder notes 'Justice'? That sounds like a vengeance motive."

"Gosh, don't ask me no more questions," grumbled Pony George. "M' head's hummin' like a hive full of bees!"

"If the killer was a member of the Toyah Lake gang an' these victims were members likewise, that vengeance motive sounds pretty strong."

"But if that murderin' hound knew the identity of his enemies," Pony George pointed out, "why should he wait fifteen year tuh knock 'em off?"

"Oh, hell," growled Lawler, disgusted. "All my figurin' travels in circles."

He resumed his restless pacing of the room, his brooding eyes passing unseeingly over its scant and roughly-made furnishings. Throwing his hat abruptly into a corner, he rumpled his sweaty, thick red hair. "This damn business is enough to tie knots in a iron bar. I reckon I oughta confess it's got me licked—but I won't. I ain't never laid down yet. George, do some thinkin' for a change!"

"*No?* Cripes, don't start pickin' on me—I don't savvy nothin' about this wave o' crime! I wa'n't cut out tuh be no Philo Vance!"

Despite the seriousness of the situation, Lawler chuckled. "I expect you spoke the truth."

Fervently he hoped the last of these murders had been committed. Up and down the room he strode, trying to find some path out of this maze of leads—some path which would bring him to the murderer and bring the murderer to the hempen noose he so richly deserved. Pony George, smoking, watched him uneasily.

Then suddenly Lawler stopped his pacing in midstride. "Lord!" he exclaimed. "What a fool I've been!"

"Wal," Pony George commented sagely, "men was borned

tuh be fools, I expect. An' women was borned tuh fool 'em."

"Listen!" Lawler's glance, as it jumped to the deputy's face, was hard as polished agate. "You've got to get right out on Reede's trail! Quick! *Wake up!* It may be too late already. God! we've blundered terrible, George!"

"Mebbe so, but yuh know I ain't much of a trailer——"

"You ain't much good sittin' round twiddlin' your thumbs or writin' poetry, either! Fork your horse pronto an' get on his trail!"

Pony George heaved a doleful sigh. "That Reede's got a awful mean pair o' eyes——"

"If you're afraid of the job, turn in your star!"

There was reproach in the chunky deputy's eyes. "It ain't that, only——"

"It looks that way to me."

"Oh! . . . Wal, if that's the way yuh feel——" Pony George shrugged, pulled his hat down aslant his eyes and with wooden face rose from his chair. "What yuh wantin' me tuh do?"

"Trail Reede. Find out where he goes an', if possible, why. See he don't get wise you're followin' him. If he looks like he's fixin' to pull his freight, clap on the bracelets an' bring him in. I think we're gonna get this thing wound up."

"Reede might not like the idee of them bracelets——"

"You got a gun. Don't be scared to use it. Whatever you do, don't let him get away!"

"All right, Red. So long."

Thrusting his cob pipe in his pocket, Pony George stepped out of the courthouse into the red gush of the dying sun's last rays and went bow-legging down the street.

Left alone, Lawler sat in gloomy silence. Pony George had said, "If thet murderin' hound knew the identity of his enemies, why should he wait fifteen years to knock 'em off?" Only one of the gang's members had ever been apprehended. That man, according to Pony George, had gone to jail, and from all the deputy knew to the contrary still was there.

"But he ain't," growled Lawler viciously. "It's damn' evident he's been let out!"

Presently the sheriff's churning thoughts reverted as they always did of late, to Sara Tranton. Despite all attempts to concentrate on the ugly business in hand, he could not put the girl from his mind, could not banish her image from his mental vision. It was there—it would not go.

Why had she turned him down? What reason could she have? What had he unwittingly done to offend her? He sighed amid the maze of questions. Answers seemed at a premium of late.

58

He reached for the phone; he'd call the Box Bar T.

It might be, he thought, that he'd find Sara in a better frame of mind than that in which he'd left her the night before. Perhaps she would tell him that she had not really meant to end their engagement permanently.

But when Sara come to the phone, she told him no such thing.

"Father isn't here right now," she said. "But I'm expecting him any minute. Could you leave a message for him? . . . Oh! you want to talk with me! But I *can't* talk right now; I'm getting supper. . . . But, if I stand here gabbing, the supper'll burn up! By the way, Red—Dad said to tell you if you called, that he spent all morning hunting for that second bullet, but did not have any luck . . . Two more killed?" he heard her gasp, then: "Yes, I'll tell him to be careful. Now I really *must* hang up—something's burning. 'Bye!"

Lawler alternately sat in glowering silence and paced in impotent anger. The world was certainly going haywire fast! Nothing came out right! He recalled a random phrase of Pony George's—"A life o' mis'ry from the cradle to the grave!" He nevertheless snorted at such foolishness. If there was something wrong between Sara and himself, he felt, the rub must be in something he had done or left undone. But thinking so gave him precious little consolation.

He put on his hat and left the office. He headed for the "Lone Star Grub Emporium." He told himself he might feel better with a little nourishment under his belt.

Being close to the border, some few of Pecos' houses housed Mexican families. Several doorways he passed as he strode along the street were filled, he saw, by sleepy-eyed *mestizo* women, resting before the necessity of cleaning up their supper dishes. Against adobe walls lolled the women's *saraped* menfolk. These roused themselves sufficently to reveal a lazy interest in the sheriff's movements. One or two murmured respectful greetings, which Lawler returned. One fellow grinned sardonically. The sheriff paid him no attention.

There were no customers in the restaurant when he entered. The regular patrons had evidently eaten their meals and gone off about their various businesses. Along one side of the place stretched a rough board counter, oilcloth-covered; at the other were a number of littered tables. Lawler took a stool at the counter.

At the rear of the restaurant the doors leading to the kitchen swung abruptly open a girl emerged. She was not bad looking. She had dark wavy hair and a complexion innocent of make-up. She had hazel eyes that smiled when they met the sheriff's.

"Hello, Red," she leaned across the counter. "Long time no see."

Lawler smiled. "I was here this noon—no, I wasn't either. Out——"

"You bet you weren't. If you'd been here I'd have waited on you. How goes the sheriff business? From things I've heard I'd say it was on the up-an'-up."

Lawler scowled. "I'll have——" he began. But a burst of silvery laughter that showed white even teeth between her vivid lips interrupted him.

Her eyes twinkled. "You want," she prophesied, "a pair of hen-fruit an' a double order of ham."

"You're a mind-reader," Lawler grinned. "What else am I wantin'?"

"A cup of java—black. An' the whole works in a hurry."

"Marv'lous." Lawler picked up a soiled copy of last Friday's paper.

As he was finishing his supper, Obe Kringle came in. The black-frocked coroner smirked at sight of the sheriff. "Well, well," he said. "Quite an inquest we had this mornin', eh?"

Lawler nodded briefly and downed the last of his coffee.

"Hope you're intendin' to put a extra guard on the jail to-night," Kringle said.

Lawler set down his empty cup. "What for?"

"I understand you put Link Holladay in jail."

"What's that got to do with it?"

"Link's a tough customer. Seems tuh me if I was you——"

"You ain't," was Lawler's curt interruption.

"You better be careful. Link Holladay's got friends. They might try to spring him."

"Are you aimin' to tell me how to run my office?"

"It's time somebody did," the coroner snapped. "Three men murdered inside of two weeks an'——"

"Listen, Kringle," Lawler's drawl was soft and cold. "It may be time I was showin' some results. I'll admit that much, in fact. But I got no call to take any back-talk outa you. What's more I ain't figurin' to. *Savvy?*"

Obe Kringle's chest expanded with importance. "See here, young fella. You can't talk to me that way. For two bits I'd have you thrown out of office!"

Lawler's extended hand showed two bits at the coroner. "You aimin' to do the throwin'?"

"By Gawd, I'm big enough!" fist drawn back and tightly balled, Kringle stepped forward threateningly. "The way you let the killer get that knife outa your office is a disgrace to Reeves County. I've got a damned good notion——"

60

"Then be kind to it," Lawler drawled, "because it's in one hell of a strange place!"

Slapping the two bits down on the counter to pay for his meal, he strode from the restaurant without a backward glance.

## Chapter XII

### THE CAPTAIN'S PHONE RINGS TWICE

RETURNING to the office Lawler flung his hat into a corner, lit the lamp above his desk and dropped disgustedly into his chair. This situation, he told himself grimly, bade fair to lick him and get him turned out of office unless he swiftly made some progress. "Sure as a Chinaman's eyes is slanted!"

He well realized that Kringle's words were but a slice of what he soon would hear on every side unless he swiftly succeeded in unmasking and capturing the man who was taking ironic pleasure in signing himself "Justice."

But how to do it? This was a tough layout, and no mistake!

Reede might be the angle by which he could crack the whole business—but, Reede had got away from town before Lawler had thought to put someone on his trail. It was very possible that Pony George would be unable to trail the man any great distance before losing "sign" completely.

If Reede was as clever as Lawler was beginning to think him——

His thought turned to Tawson. Like Reede, Tawson employed no hands on his spread. Like Reede, too, Tawson tended such stock as he had himself and only bothered with his cattle when they seemed in danger of wandering off. More than once Lawler had thought it strange Link Holladay's long-loopers had not gobbled up these two small herds. Perhaps their mediocrity alone protected them.

What Tawson and Reede did with the bulk of their time few persons in the vicinity had any notion. Tawson, Lawler supposed, spent most of his leisure on looking into the thing he had been sent out here to investigate. But if he were being more successful at it than Lawler, the sheriff felt the man deserved a danged sight more than he was getting for the work.

What Reede did with *his* spare time, Lawler had no idea— up to the present, that is to say. Right now he had a mighty dark suspicion.

Reede had appeared in the country about three months

61

previously, mounted on a flea-bitten horse and appearing much the same as he now looked. His marked pallor would have been cause for interested speculation on the part of his neighbours, had it not been self-evident that he was slowly dying from consumption.

Reede claimed to have hailed from Colorado, but his speech and manner belied the claim. His was the soft drawl of the Texan and his ungainly, slouching walk would have branded him Texan in any Colorado gathering. Lawler was wondering if the past fifteen years of Reede's life might not account for the man's lie, when the telephone on his desk awoke with a hoarse, insistent jangle. Picking up the instrument, Lawler scooped the receiver to his ear and into the mouthpiece growled:

"Red Lawler speakin'."

It was Pony George. "Listen, Red. I got on to Reede's trail all right. But I lost him headin' fer the Bar 2."

Lawler scowled. "Lost him, eh? Where you at now?"

"Tawson's."

"Tawson there?"

"No—nor Reede, neither. No hosses in the corral an' only one in the stable. Tawson's got two so I reckon he must be out prowlin' someplace. Listen: what do yuh want I should do now? Want me tuh wait here an' see if Reede comes?"

"No. He won't show up at Tawson's. Use your head f'r change! Get over to the Lazy R an' if Reede ain't there, wait until he comes. See that you get your bronc put outa sight so's he won't know you're around. An' listen to me, George; once you pick Reede up, you be damn well sure he doesn't give you the slip a second time."

"Hey—hold on a sec, Red! Where yuh gunna be, case I wanta call yuh?"

"I'll be out to Tranton's. You can get me there in about an hour."

Lawler hung up and strode across the room to retrieve his hat, little guessing that crouched in the black shadows outside the open windows a man stood tensely listening. The eyes behind his sleepy lids were concealed by the down-turned brim of a black Stetson. There was a grin upon his parted lips—but not a pretty thing to see.

Picking up his hat, Lawler closed the office door behind him and went striding down the corridor, spur-chains jingling musically.

Outside the courthouse beneath the star-filled heavens, he lost no time stepping into the saddle atop his big roan gelding. Picking up the reins he kneed the willing animal

forward, swinging him into a lope a short time later on the
trail that led past the Box Bar T.

Save for the pounding of the gelding's hoofs the night's
vast silence seemed absolute.

Red and fat, the moon crept above the distant eastern
skyline with the slow solemnity of a royal progress. The
stars blinked balefully as the glowing disc ascended; showed
the sandy trail twisting between intermittent borders of
desert growth. Occasionally a gnarled juniper reared its
bleached and splintery form in lonely solitude beside the way.
Rabbit brush and mesquite stretched away on either side.

As he neared the Box Bar T, Red Lawler was recalling the
eager expectancy which had flooded through him last night
as he approached this place. Before the veranda he stepped
from the saddle and left the gelding with trailing reins.
Sara stood watching him from the doorway. Never, he felt,
would he be able to understand the strange moods that
swayed her mind and governed her inexplicable actions.

Yet he could not but admire her lithe and graceful form
as she stood there outlined against the lamplight streaming
from the hall.

"What is it, Red?"

The lack of emotion in her low voice struck against the
denied yearning of young Lawler with definite impact. It
was almost a minute before he replied. Then he said, "Too
cold out here for you without no coat. Let's get inside."

Sara listlessly led the way into the big sitting room. It
was across the hall from the Captain's office. She took a
chair that placed her back to the light, thus discounting
at the start the revealing mobility of her piquant features.
Lawler stood, hat in hand, beside the door.

"I asked you not to call again, Red."

Lawler fidgeted with his hat. "Well, er, it's 'fficial business,
Sara . . ."

"What do you mean, 'official'?"

"I come over," Red lied, "to talk with your Dad about
that second bullet."

There might have been read in her glance at that moment
a strange look of mingled pity and longing, a wistful combination that did not harmonize with her words—a look
Red Lawler could not see because of the light that was
behind her on the table.

Her gaze rested long upon his clean-shaven, aquiline
features beneath the tousled red hair. It seemed as though she
might be studying his face and striving to impress it on
her memory that she might recall its detail later. If so, she
could not have failed to note that the usual glint of humour

63

was totally absent from his eyes: that there were new, grim lines about his tight-lipped mouth. Indeed she must have seen and steeled her heart against him, for her voice was cold:

"I told you last night it would be foolish to keep this up. I'm not in love with you, nor you with me. That infatuation that we felt for one another now is dead. It won't be rekindled. There can be nothing more between us, Red. I—I think you'd better go."

For long moments he stared, then a cold oath dropped from his lips. "So you're throwin' me down! That's final, eh?"

In the light of the lamp behind her he saw her head nod once. A grim, dogged stubbornness crept into the forward throw of his jaw as the poignant silence threatened to become insupportable.

A chill wind was rising off the desert; it soughed eerily through the dust-coated branches of the cottonwoods and pig-locusts and rattled loose panes in the windows. The creak and clatter of the windmill was plainly audible. In her lap Sara's hands nervously twisted a fold in her skirt. Her glance appeared to study the pattern of the worn carpet on the floor.

"Well, I ain't figurin' to take it as final," Lawler growled. "You ain't given me no reason for breaking things off like this. You——"

"I don't intend to say any more on the subject!" Sara's chin could show stubbornness, too.

"Like that, eh?"

"Yes."

"Seems like you're gettin' kinda penickety when the sheriff of Reeves County ain't good enough for you."

"It isn't the sheriff so much as it is the pay he draws."

"What's the matter with it?"

"It's too meagre to support a wife as I wish to be supported."

Lawler stared. Certainly this was a side of the Captain's daughter he had not been privileged to see before. "It's a heap better'n cowpuncher pay."

"But we're not discussing cowpunchers and I'm not expecting to marry one."

"We ain't discussin' much of anythin', if you're askin' me!"

"Well, there's nothing left to discuss. I told you not to come out here again."

"I don't get this, Sara. I don't get it a-tall! It ain't like you to act this way. If your ol' man don't want me for a son-in-law, quit beatin' round the bush an' say so."

"The Captain hasn't anything to do with this matter."

64

Lawler thought he detected a flush of colour in her cheeks but could not be sure because of that cussed light behind her. To him her face was hardly more than a vague oval with radiant golden hair. "Really," she was saying, "I don't care to talk about it longer."

"All right." There was a new, cold bleakness in the sheriff's voice—it was like the crunch of wagon wheels on frozen snow. "Last night you said you'd heard the sound of running feet after them gunshots. You seemed to think they was movin' towards the house. Don't you reckon mebbe the angle from which you caught the sound made it seem like that, while actually the sound was movin' *away?*"

"I suppose so. The wind was blowing. It was almost impossible to tell anything definite about it. I was merely giving an impression when I told you that. My father——"

"Captain's explanation," he cut in, "described the sound as that of a runnin' horse. *He* seemed to think it was the sniper forkin' his bronc away."

"Well? Probably that is the way it was."

"What?"

"A horseman moving off."

"Oh." He bent a bleak look upon her. But he had little success in making out her expression with that light before his eyes. Thrusting his hands deep-down in his pockets he took a turn or two about the room.

"Did you hear a galloping horse?"

"I don't know what I heard!" she exclaimed defiantly. "It was on the other side of the house, whatever it was. I wasn't expecting to hear anything and didn't pay much attention to it when I did hear it. What difference does it make? The main thing now, it seems to me, is to see to it no one tries to shoot Dad a second time."

Lawler's eyes were a jade-like, fathomless green; baffling, mocking.

She lashed out at him, "If you want to help us, why don't you send Pony George out here to see that no further attempts are——"

"Does the Captain want Pony George out here?"

"Of course he doesn't. He's got men of his own, if he wants to bring them in off the range. But he makes light of the whole business—tries to make me think it was hardly worth mentioning. Just a crazy drunken cowboy antic. But I know better." Her voice rose fierce with passionate protest. "Half an inch to the left and that shot would have killed him!"

"I don't reckon you'd have been so upset if it had been me," he said sardonically. "Where's the Captain now?"

"I think you'd better be going," she said.

"I expect there ain't any great hurry. I'm waitin' for a call from Pony George."

"Where is he?"

"Bein' that George's whereabouts ain't got nothin' to do with your precious father," growled Lawler bitterly, "I don't guess you'd be a heap interested."

She flared up like tow. "My father has been mighty good to me—a sight better than you could *ever* be! I've never wanted a thing he hasn't gotten me. There is nothing he would not do for me——"

"That's what's the matter with you," Lawler cut in drily. "You been spoiled. What you need's a damn' good spankin'!"

Her breath was drawn in sharply. She surged from her chair and crossed the room to stand rigid beside the window, staring stormily out at the windy night.

"Get away from that window!" Lawler snapped.

She half turned her head and Lawler saw that her eyes were bright with anger. "This happens to be my house and your jurisdiction does not extend inside it. I'll do as I please. And if it doesn't suit you, Red Lawler, you can take yourself off any time you see fit!"

Lawler's red hair got the best of him, then.

"You little fool!" In three strides he was across the room. His big hands caught her by the shoulders, jerked her back from the window. "Ain't you got no sense a-tall?" He shook her roughly so that her teeth chattered and her golden hair came down about her face and shoulders. "Don't you know better'n to stand in front of a lighted window? You figurin' to get yourself killed?"

Colour blazed against the paleness of her cheeks. Lawler saw that her lower lip was trembling. But whether these were signs of anger, shame, or fear, he could not tell. All he knew was that her beauty caused a dull pounding in his breast, a constriction of his throat.

He stepped closer till her eyes came up and stopped him. Deep brown they were, and just now bright and sparkly.

"Sara," he said, and paused, confused by the searching scrutiny of her glance.

"Well?" she seemed throbbing with emotion. "Make your apology and go."

"I've no apology to make," he said, and squared his shoulders stubbornly. "If there's an apology due, I expect it's comin' to me. Anyway, I'm not pullin' out till I hear from George."

"I can't see why he should call you here. Or any other place, for that matter."

"I expect there's a lot of things you don't see," he told her flatly.

"Where is Pony George? Why does he have to call you?"

"Where's the Captain?" Lawler countered.

"The movements of Pony George are mighty secret," she sneered.

"The movements of Pony George are the business of the Sheriff's office, an' I'm not aimin' to broadcast 'em to the general public. This county's had four murders now since I took oath of office, an' I ain't figurin' to have a fifth."

"Four!"

"So that gives you a jolt, does it? Well it jolted me too. The next jolt's comin' to that killer when he finds me starin' at him down the barrel of a gun!"

But she was not listening, he saw. There was an added brightness in her eyes, an added pallor to her cheeks.

"Doak and Toreva——" her voice grew breathless. "Who are the others?"

"A gent called Max Smith an' that big-eared fella over at Barstow."

"Smith and Lester." She was staring at him fixedly. "Who's Smith?"

"A driftin' pilgrim that's dropped his picket pin permanent."

"Where was——"

"No use your askin' me any more questions," Lawler cut in gruffly. "The Sheriff of Reeves County ain't no information bureau. I'm goin' to get that killer an get him quick. He won't get another chance at Captain Dan, so quit lookin' at me so funny-like."

"Was I?" she crossed to the table, stood looking down at the lamp. "You'd put duty to your office above every other consideration—above personal danger, for instance?"

"Of course—what kind of an officer would I be if I didn't? Naturally, I put my duty first. I swore to do that when I took my oath of office."

She nodded as though to something in her mind. She gave no sign of hearing him, but said, "Duty and loyalty are fine things, I guess. Dad's like that, too. Unswervable as granite."

"Sure," Lawler agreed. "He learned that captaining his ships. What kind of a skipper would he have been if he'd spent all his time worrying about his own neck an' the awful chances he'd be takin' in every storm an' fog? It's a mighty poor specimen of a man who ain't willin' to lay down his life in the performance of what he conceives to be his duty."

"Then you'd put loyalty to your office—what you conceive to be your duty," Sara asked listlessly, "before every other consideration?"

He nodded emphatically.

"And in the case of Dad captaining a ship . . . you'd

expect him to stay with a ship he knew was sinking—even though it cost him his life—purely out of respect and loyalty to his owners?"

"If that would be his duty—sure. I'd certainly expect that from a man like Captain Dan."

She nodded slowly, reluctantly, it seemed. Her shoulders seemed to droop a little. When she spoke, so softly were the words sent forth that he could hardly catch them: "Duty and loyalty must be very dear to a man, I think."

"I'll say this," remarked Lawler grimly. "When you broke off our engagement I was powerfully astonished. I sure hadn't expected anythin' like that from you. I thought you had a lot of loyalty in *your* make-up. Shows how a fella——"

"I don't guess we need bring that up again," she cut in smoothly, and turned to rearrange her dishevelled hair. "You've worn that subject pretty thin."

For a second Lawler glared, and then: "Where's Captain Dan?" he demanded gruffly.

"He went to town right after supper."

"What for?"

"I didn't ask him."

A hard, brittle silence fell between them. Sara sat by the table, busy with her hair, ignoring Lawler completely. He stood against the wall near the window, his hands in his pockets, a look of resentment in his brooding eyes.

Presently, from the Captain's office, came the jangle of the telephone.

Sara started for the door with quickened stride, but Lawler got there first. "I'll take it," he said shortly, and passed out into the hall. Sara pressed close behind.

Entering the Captain's office, Lawler grabbed up the phone. He held the receiver against his ear. Yet Sara, standing close, could hear nearly as well as he. It was Pony George, and the deputy's voice was loud with excitement.

"I got here a bit too late, Red——"

"Where are you?" Lawler growled with a scowl at the listening Sara.

"Lazy R, of course. But I didn't get here quick enough— Reede's cashed his chips! Killer sifted him s' full of holes yuh couldn't float him in a bucket of brine! I found one of them notes on him—one of them 'Justice' things."

"Read it!"

"It says: 'Only the wise an' the dead keep motionless tongues.' What yuh s'pose he means by that? Yuh don't reckon yuh coulda learned what Reede let slip as he left our office, do yuh? Say—want I should bring the body back tuh town?"

"Never mind the body," growled Lawler grimly. "Get

busy an' search his clothes. Search the whole place while you're about it! Grab everything you can find relatin' to the Toyah Lake gang. Call me back when you're finished searchin'. I'll wait here till I hear from you."

Sara saw that his hand was shaking as he returned the receiver to its hook. And small wonder, she thought. The strain, together with the unsolvable aspect of these murders, was enough to wrench anyone's nerves. More than enough if the man were the sheriff. This business was taking toll of Lawler. Each passing hour new lines of strain and worry etched deeper into the bronze of his face. She would have felt sorry for him had it not been for the viewpoint he had so forcibly expressed.

She saw a strange, intent, startled light abruptly flare in the depths of his deep green glance. She watched him lower his weight heavily to the Captain's desk, watched his lips grow tight and grim.

Several moments he sat there rigid as Sara stared at him. Slowly he seemed to grow aware of her glance. A dark wave of colour crept up behind the bronze of his cheeks. And then the phone beside him jangled loudly.

## Chapter XIII

### PONY GEORGE MAKES A DISCOVERY

IN the single room of the shack at Bar 2, an unpretentious structure intended originally for a line camp but promoted by its present owner to the dignity of being styled a ranch house, Pony George put down the phone with a sigh of genuine relief. The expected fireworks had not materialised. For Red Lawler, the sheriff, had been quite mild, his deputy reflected, merely ordering him to proceed to the Lazy R and await the coming of Reede.

Pony George felt no call to hurry. "Rome wa'n't built in no day!" he muttered, and proceeded to look around.

The furnishings with which Tawson had equipped the Bar 2 shack were simple. A dishevelled pile of blankets covered the single bunk against the far wall. Above this rustic pallet was a bracket lamp with a tin reflector and, tacked to the hand-hewn logs beside it, the picture of a nude dancer clipped from some lewd magazine. Suspended from the opposite wall by a thick wooden peg hung a silver-mounted saddle, its black leather bright and shiny in the light from the kerosene lamp. A pail of water with a dipper stood beside the door. Across from the bunk was a chair on which reposed a battered clock and a tiny pad of yellow paper.

A burly man with smouldering eyes in a high-boned face the colour of mahogany stepped suddenly into the room, softly closing the door behind him. A pair of black-butted six-shooters swung at his hips.

Pony George looked up with a start from the engrossing task of examining more closely the pad of yellow paper. "Gosh!" he spluttered. "Whyn't yuh scare a man tuh death an' be done with it?"

The smouldering eyes of Buck Tawson raked the shack's interior with a sweeping, comprehensive glance. "Did I scare yuh? Must have a guilty conscience."

"Guilty, hell! For a fella of yore weight yuh sure can move uncommon silent!"

"That's the Indian in me croppin' out. 'D you put that pad of yeller paper on that chair, George?"

"Huh? . . . No—course I didn't. D'yuh think I'm Santy Claus?"

"Funny how it got there, then."

"Why? Ain't it yores?"

"It certainly ain't," said Tawson grimly. "Never saw it before. Looks like you might not be the only visitor I've had to-night. Let's see . . ." he stepped across to the chair and gingerly picked up the object under discussion. Holding it at various angles, his smouldering eyes suddenly became intent and he stepped closer to the lamp. One more swift look he gave the pad then, fumbling in his pockets, he produced a pencil.

"Someone wrote somethin' on a sheet of this then tore it off," he said, and there was about him the air of a person having made a discovery. "There's a faint impression of the writin' on this top sheet."

"Bravo!" cried Pony George. "Spurlock Holmes in person! What's it say?"

Tawson's smouldering eyes gave the chunky deputy an enigmatic glance. "I can't make it out—yet. I'll try an' bring it out by rubbin' this pencil across it."

Suiting his actions to the words the marshal began lightly rubbing his pencil point across the paper's indentations. Gradually the pencil's strokes grew heavier and heavier.

A scowl creased the dried-apple countenance of Pony George. "Hell! Yuh've lost 'er now, complete!"

"You ain't tellin' me a thing," growled Tawson, and thrust the pad and pencil into a vest pocket. "Did you come out here to see me?"

"Do yuh think I'd travel this far on a chilly night jest

70

fer a squint at yore homely mug?" demanded George. "I'm here on official business. I'm trailin' a gent."

"Yeah? I guess you ain't scuffin' up his heels any, are yuh?"

Pony George ignored this thrust. "My horse needs rest."

"This ain't no halfway station." Tawson picked up his clock, shook it, listened and proceeded to give it a belated winding. "Got any notion what time it is?"

Pony George glared. "I wish tuh hell yuh could shut up fer about five seconds. Yuh got more damn lip than a muley cow! I had a swell verse right on the edge of m' tongue, an' yuh went an' scairt 'er plumb away!"

"Verse?"

Pony George glared. "Yeah—v-e-r-s-e: VERSE! I'm writin' a poem called 'The Ballad of Kyote Cal.' It's a pistol—yuh wanta hear it?"

Tawson shook his head. "I ain't strong on poetry. Didn't you say you was supposed to be trailin' a gent?"

"I don't see how yuh ever got tuh be a marshal! Y'ain't got a lick o' sense! I can trail gents any day in the week, fella; but bursts of inspiration is powerful rare events!" Scowling, the chunky deputy rose to his feet. "Yuh've scairt the muse plumb tuh Halifax now. I might's well be joggin' on Napoleon as settin' here gassin' with the likes of you."

"Napoleon!" Tawson guffawed. "Bone Rack would be a dang sight more fittin' name for the crowbait you're forkin'!"

"I've been told Napoleon had some bony parts," snapped George, and with a tug at his hat went striding outside. As he was swinging into the saddle Tawson came out, still chuckling. "I might's well ride along with you, I reckon. Where you goin'?"

"Lazy R," growled Pony George, and kicked Napoleon urgently in the ribs.

For some while they rode in silence, only the soft thudding of their horses' hoofs in the sandy soil disturbing the vast silence that cloaked the land. Even the noises of the night creatures seemed strangely hushed, as though before the majesty of the Law. Above their heads millions of stars twinkled like guttering candles in the purple bowl of night, and almost directly over them the moon, filled to yellow roundness, drifted lazily along.

"Fine night for a murder," offered Tawson, conversationally.

Pony George sniffed. "Fer company," he said, "yuh're about as cheerful as a graveyard. Don't yuh never think of nothin' but murder, gunfights an' brawls?"

"Sure—once in a while I think of jails an' scaffolds an' hangmen's ropes."

Conversation lapsed.

A short distance to the north they could see the dark smear of trees marking the length of Toyah Lake. To the southwest, behind them, the dark bulk of Newman Peak blotted out a section of stars along the skyline. The downslanting moonlight picked out the gear metal of their mounts' trappings and was reflected from the badge on the vest of Pony George, and from the shoulder-plates of the rifles that were sheathed in their saddle scabbards.

A wind seemed to have abruptly risen, cold and penetrating. It created an eery swishing in the chaparral and soughed unpleasantly in the deputy's ears.

"Mebbe we better move a bit faster," he muttered presently. "Red's expectin' me tuh call him, come tuh think of it. Le's lope awhile."

From time to time he threw a sidelong glance at Tawson as they rode with heads bent against the wind. But he could not read the man's expression; his face, though turned to Pony George, was but a vague oval in the half-light.

Eight miles it was from Tawson's Bar 2 to Reede's Lazy R —a mere stone's throw as distances are measured in the West. In the daytime one ranch could easily be seen by a person at the other; that is, the clump of trees shading its buildings could be seen. Even now they could see the trees at the Lazy R, but only as a dark blur against the lighter colour of the sand.

A half hour passed to the steady beating of the horses' hoofs and the pounding of the animals' hearts against their riders' knees.

"Colder'n a well-chain in February, ain't it?"

"A little chilly," Tawson admitted briefly.

Odd about that pad of paper, Pony George was thinking. If it was not Tawson's how had it come to be in Tawson's shack? That it had been generously left there by someone else sounded rather thin to the chunky deputy. If it *was* Tawson's, why had he sought to establish it as the property of someone else?

A coyote's dismal yammer came wailing across the wind.

"Bad omen, that," growled Tawson grimly.

"Yuh're sure one happy jasper!" George grunted. "Reg'lar li'l ray of sunshine, ain't yuh?"

From the south came mournfully the deep answering howl of a lobo.

"All we need now," spluttered Pony George, "is a corpse tuh make the evenin' a huge success!"

The night was shimmering with tiny silver gleams where the moonglare lay upon the lake when the two lawmen arrived at the Lazy R. Pulling his horse in behind the stable where lay thick shadows, the marshal asked, "What you figgerin' to do now?"

"Dunno," admitted Pony George, glancing round apprehensively. "I expect we better leave the nags here an' go on up to the house. What's yore idee?"

Tawson shrugged. "Mebbe we better squint inside this stable first. See if the blue roan's here."

"Why the—Say! How'd yuh know he was ridin' the roan to-night?"

"Saw 'im leavin' town this afternoon 'fore supper."

"Was yuh in town?"

"How else?"

"Wal, unless yuh was there round supper time as well, I don't sabe how yuh could see Reede pullin' out. S'far as *I* know, Reede didn't leave till nearly dark."

"Expect you don't know everything," Tawson's tone was curt. Ground-hitching his horse, he strode round to the stable door and went inside. Grumbling, Pony George followed.

Inside Tawson struck a match. It burst purple and yellow against the hovering shadows. Reede's blue roan was in a stall munching oats contentedly.

"Reckon Reede's home," Tawson said, and led the way from the stable. "Funny he ain't got a light on."

"Mebbe he's gone to bed," suggested Pony George dubiously. "He might have, yuh know. I suppose the fella sleeps sometimes."

"Sure—daytimes."

"Yuh seem to know a powerful lot about Reede's business."

"Ought to. I been keepin' my eye on 'im," Tawson said. "He's one of the ol' Toyah Lake gang—the only one that ever got sent up. Took the rap under the handle of Tim Rein. He got released six months ago f' good behaviour an' because he'd developed consumption an' woulda passed out if they'd kep' him in much longer."

An exclamation of astonishment escaped the chunky deputy. "Didn't he ever squeal on the rest of the gang?"

"Nope. You got to give him credit f' that. He kep' his mouth shut tight."

Approaching the ranch house they stepped into the murky shadows obscuring the porch. Their spurs rang loudly as they crossed it to knock upon the door. The might have saved themselves the bother, for no answer came. The creaking of the windmill and the rattling of the windows made the only sound.

This place of Reede's was a small adobe, one story high, with a flat adobe roof—its mud plastered over cedar logs whose ends projected a foot or so over the front and rear walls. There might be three rooms within, George thought; a large front room with a kitchen and bedroom at the rear.

Tawson knocked again and called Reede's name. Still no answer came. And no faintest sound of inside movement betrayed a person's presence. Tawson opened the door. Pony George crowded in behind him. Through an uncurtained window came sufficient radiance from the moon to disclose a lamp upon a table. Tawson lifted its chimney and struck a match. When he replaced the chimney he and Pony George glanced round. They were in the main room of the ex-convict's establishment and saw that, though scantily furnished, the place was neat and clean.

In the room's rear wall were two closed doors bearing out Pony George's surmise. "Bring the light," he growled, approaching them. "He's prob'ly sleepin' back here."

"He's probably," said Tawson, picking up the lamp, "saddled another bronc an' gone for a ride."

The first door tried led to the kitchen. A hasty glance sufficed to show that no one sat in the chair drawn up beside the stove.

Returning to the main room, Tawson held the lamp above his head while Pony George grasped the knob of the second door with the intention of continuing the search. But it was not to be that easy. This door, he found, was locked. He bent down and put his eye to the keyhole, but the only thing he discovered was that the key had been removed.

"Reckon yuh was right," he said, straightening. "The door's locked an' the key ain't in it so it looks like he mighta took a ride, like yuh said. Can't figger why he'd wanta lock the door though. Must have somethin' valu'ble in there."

Tawson scowled. "I doubt it. Here—hold the lamp."

Pony George had the lamp in his hands before he realized that Tawson had usurped his place as boss. Resentfully he watched the marshal hurl his burly shoulder against the door. His first onslaught split a panel in its upper half. "Some brawn!" thought George, and was glad it had not been *his* shoulder which had dealt the splintering blow. Another lunge and the battered door cracked open. Tawson kicked the hanging wood aside and entered. Pony George followed with the lamp.

He nearly dropped the lamp when his startled eyes took in the contents of the room. A muttered prayer slipped past his lips. For a bed occupied the room's centre and face-down across it lay a moveless form—a man's! Rusty black clothes hung limply to his bony frame. The back of his head was smashed and blood was on the bed-sheets.

"Is—is he dead?" gasped Pony George.

74

"If he ain't," Tawson's humour was grim, "the undertaker'll be playin' him a dirty trick!"

George shivered. "Who done it?"

"I wouldn't know. Better call the coroner."

"I better call Red Lawler first . . ."

Setting the lamp on the floor Pony George clumped back to the front room. After a brief search he found the telephone box, and just as he did Tawson called:

"There's a note on him, George. Says 'Only the wise an' the dead keep motionless tongues.' It's signed 'Justice,' like them others."

When Pony George put down the phone, with Lawler's instructions still ringing in his ears, Tawson came slowly from the bedroom carrying the lamp. He set it down on the table and buttoned up his coat.

"Reckon I'll be moseyin' along, George. See yuh later, mebbe."

"What's yore hurry, fella? I got no special hankerin' tuh be stayin' here alone with Reede's corpse."

"Tough. But I got other fish to fry," said Tawson, grining. "S'long."

And why Pony George watched him resentfully, Buck Tawson—who had introduced himself to the Sheriff's office as a U.S. Marshal—jingled his spurs across the room and out the door. Some moments later diminishing hoofbeats announced the departure of a horse.

Pony George swore with feeling. "He sure was in some lather tuh get away from here! Fella with his gloomy disposishun oughta feel right tuh home in such surroundin's. Dang 'im, anyway!" He stared apprehensively about. "I never did pretend tuh be no Spurlock Holmes," he muttered. "Nor did I ever have any leanin' towards the undertakin' business. Cripes, I gotta notion tuh pull outa here myself!"

He threw a narrowed glance around him, searching out the shadows. But he saw nothing to alarm him. Despite this fact he pulled the heavy six-shooter from his holster and examined its chamber carefully. Having done so, he retained the weapon in his hand.

Lawler had told him definitely to search this place for clues. Well, he would—so long as such a search did not involve returning to the bedroom. So, one eye peeled for likely hiding places, one eye keening the hovering shadows, Pony George began his probing.

He kept to the open places as much as he could. He preferred to search where the lamplight shone the brightest. Thus it was that upon the wall above the telephone box he became aware of a large calendar. And seeing it, his attention became suddenly gripped.

Yet because of his rising interest in the calendar, he failed to see or hear the burly form of a crouching man who moved across the porch with catlike steps to pause in the open door.

The calendar that held Pony George's attention was a large ornate affair, decorated with the picture of a chorus girl in colours. Still it was not her buxom charms so flashily displayed that held George's wondering gaze.

It was the four tacks, one at each of the calendar's corners, holding the thing to the wall that drew his interest.

"No need of *four* tacks tuh hold that thing up," he muttered thoughtfully. "One tack driven through the eye at the top would do the trick." Out of curiosity he ripped the calendar from the two tacks that held its lower edge against the wall. An envelope dropped to the floor. Picking it up George thrust his gun in the waistband of his trousers. Though having been through the mails, the envelope was no longer sealed so George felt no compunction in removing from it a twice-folded sheet of yellow paper. He unfolded it with trembling fingers, so great was his mounting interest upon noting its colour.

One swift glance he gave the pencilled lines. With an oath he grabbed the phone-box crank and twirled it wildly. Those pencilled lines had read:

> "I'll see that you get your share of the loot
> if you sit tight and keep yore lip buttoned."

A single initial was used for signature; though blurred, Pony George guessed the letter instantly.


## Chapter XIV

### "THE CARDS IS DEALT"

As Lawler swung round on the Captain's desk, reaching for the phone, it seemed that all sound throughout the house had abruptly become suspended; all sound save the solitary ticking of a clock.

Feeling Sara's eyes upon him Lawler clapped the receiver to his ear. "Well," he growled, "spit it out, George."

The receiver made metallic noises; Lawler said "Oh!" real odd, added a hurried "Thanks" and hung up. He looked at

Sara. "Wasn't George—it was the jailer at Pecos. Link Holladay's slipped his picket pin."

Sara stared at him strangely, he thought. "You mean he's got away?" A dry little sob escaped her lips as he nodded.

"Lord, Sara——" Lawler was off the desk and by her side. But she waved him back.

"I'm all right, Red. Just a little unstrung, I guess. What," she cleared her throat, "did you mean about him getting away? Away from what? He wasn't in jail, was he?"

"He sure was. I put him there yesterday durin' the inquest on Toreva. There was some evidence against him in connection with the fella's killin'."

"When did he get out?"

"Jailer didn't seem to know. He'd been off to visit his sick wife. When he got back he recalled he had a prisoner and got some supper for him at the restaurant. But when he went to the cell, Holladay was gone."

"How could——"

But his raised hand stopped her question. "You're gonna say 'How could he be guilty of killin' Toreva—he hardly knew the Mexican.' But—a blackjack with Link's name burned on the handle was found under one of the windows in the room where we found Toreva's body. Toreva had been struck across the head with some blunt instrument. The blow caused a fracture of the parietal bone."

"But Link Holladay didn't kill Toreva—surely he didn't. You can't hold him for it; he's innocent!"

"Yeah. Seems like that was the opinion of the coroner's jury, too. They," he added drily, "turned in a verdict of murder by parties unknown."

"But can't you see, Red? Someone is trying to frame him—trying to shift their own guilt on to his shoulders." Deep feeling came into her tones:

"He's not guilty, Red. He can't be."

"You ain't heard all the evidence. Big-Ear Lester claims he saw a man sneakin' out Toreva's back gate last night. Time's about right, near as we can tell. Lester claims the man was Holladay; he doesn't swear to it, but he seems pretty sure." In a moment he added softly, "Lester describes him as a big fellow—heavy-set."

"But can't you see? " she pleaded desperately. "That almost proves they're trying to frame him. I tell you, Link Holladay is no more guilty of killing Toreva than I am."

Lawler eyed her grimly. "Kinda interested in Link, ain't yuh?"

"Don't be silly! I don't want to see a man accused of something he didn't do! And if that jury did not bring in a verdict against him you've no right to hold him!"

"I ain't," he drawled. "He's departed."

"Then let him go. Forget about him."

"Mmm-m-m. How 'bout that blackjack? You want I should forget that, too?"

"Who found it?"

"Obe Kringle."

Her lip curled with disdain. "I wouldn't trust Mr. Kringle any farther than I could see him."

"Don't know's I would, either," Lawler answered. "But I don't reckon I'd go so far's to say Obe planted that evidence deliberate."

"Somebody did."

"Did what?"

Her brown eyes flashed. "It isn't fair to hound a man like that!"

For several minutes they eyed one another steadily, appraisingly; green glance probing into brown glance. Brown eyes staring back unwavering.

Sara asked, "How did he get away?"

"Jailer didn't know. Said Kringle visited right after I left the office, but that Kringle left before he did."

"Was Link there when Kringle visited——" Sara stopped abruptly, but Lawler caught her meaning.

"You mean did the jailer get a look at Link while Kringle was visiting? Hmm. I dunno. I didn't think to ask. But it's a damn good point!"

"But Kringle wouldn't have let him out after all the work he went to to put him in there," Sara protested. "Maybe the jailer——"

"I think not, though of course it's possible. In my opinion the coroner fixed Link's getaway."

"Why?"

"Obe an' me passed a few words at the Lone Star Grub to-night. He told me like he was bossin' the job I better put a extra guard round the jail. I couldn't see it. Kringle said some of Link's friends would be makin' a try to spring him."

Lawler paused, as though scanning something in his mind, then added:

"Obe's the sort of gent who'd do anything that might be expected to put me in bad with the voters. I wouldn't put it past him to have helped Link out, even though he is the one who put Link in. I'll admit, however, that I have no definite knowledge that Link was still in jail when Obe came over. I thought he was. But he might have gotten loose while I was still in town."

"But wouldn't you have known it?"

"I haven't visited the cells since noon. Link's the only prisoner I had. I expected the jailer to feed him——"

"Red," Sara broke in, "why don't you resign?"

"What?" Lawler laughed shortly. "Throw up the job just when I'm about to put the rope round the killer's neck? Humph! I guess not, Sara. Seems like I ain't in a real good givin'-up mood, this evenin'."

For several seconds the room was silent. Then, drawling, Lawler asked:

"Who was here to-night to see the Captain?"

"Who was here?" she echoed.

"Yeah—who?"

"Mister Tawson came over from the Bar 2 for a short time after supper. He and Dad left together." She eyed him anxiously. "What makes you ask? Do you think Link Holladay had been here?"

"No, I didn't expect Link had been here. I don't expect him to come within miles of here to-night. I——"

"What are you going to do about him?"

"Do about him?" Lawler looked blank.

"You know what I mean. What are you going to do about him breaking jail?"

"Why are you so anxious about him?"

Her lips quivered. She was facing the light and her eyes held an odd, sort of anxious expression. He thought it was the expression of a woman, sorely troubled, striving to remain courageous despite the crushing force of some black thing aligned against her.

She finally shrugged and turned away without speaking.

Lawler watched her, his hands deep-thrust in his Levis pockets, big shoulders hunched a little forward, his eyes brooding.

He took a turn about the room, paused before the windows and drew their shades down level with the sills.

"What's that for?"

"I got no hankerin' to get shot," he answered bluntly. "Did the Cap'n find where that second bullet struck?"

One hand went to her lips; her eyes went wide with some unreadable emotion.

And abruptly Lawler, watching her, laughed. A short and bitter laugh it was, and rang jarringly across the sullen stillness.

Sara sprang forward. "Red——"

But he held her off. "Never mind," he growled. "That second shot struck there!" he jabbed a finger at the splintered hole in the polished surface of Dan Tranton's desk. "Yeah—right there!"

"But—but that's where the first bullet hit . . ."

"Oh, no it ain't! The second bullet drilled that hole. An' I believe you know it!"

"No, no, *no!*" Sara retreated before the light in Lawler's eyes. Retreated until her back was against the farther wall. "The first shot——"

"Quit lyin' to me, Sara! I know where the first slug struck. That hole in the desk was made by the second."

She huddled against the wall, silent, trembling; stark misery in her glance.

"By Gawd," Lawler snarled, "I believe I know who this blasted killer is!"

"Red!" Sara's broken cry seemed wrung from her very soul. "Give up this awful job—Turn in your star to-night and I'll go with you anywhere! I'll marry you——"

While she was speaking it seemed for a moment that Red Lawler was going to yield. It was the squaring of his jaw in stubborn grimness that stopped her voice.

He shook his head. "No use. The cards is dealt, Sara. We got to play our hands."

At that moment the phone on the desk rang loudly.

Picking up the receiver Lawler pressed it to his ear. The voice coming over the wire was that of Pony George and its timbre was surcharged with a wild excitement.

"That you, Red? Wal, listen—I found a note here in a envelope. It was tucked behind a calendar. Envelope's been through the mail the twenty-third of las' month. Reede's the bird that went tuh the Big House under the name of Tim Rein. The note in this envelope's on yeller paper like them 'Justice' notes was writ on——"

"What name's signed to it?" Lawler barked.

"Note says Reede'll get his cut if——"

"*Whose name is signed to it?*" Lawler snarled, exasperated.

"No name's signed to it. The signature is a T——"

Pony George's voice was abruptly drowned in the sound of a shot. A second, third and fourth concussion smashed out in swift succession from that room at the line's far end. Tingling from the metallic vibrations, Lawler's ears scarcely heard the thud of a falling body. But he caught the mocking laugh that followed before the line went dead and its sound closed icy fingers about his heart.

Sara sank against him as he relinquished the phone. "Wh—what happened?"

She was shaking as though with cold when Lawler looked down into her white face.

There was a smothered feeling in Lawler's throat, in his mouth was the taste of brass. Staring down into her pitiful upturned face Lawler's eyes went bleak. No longer was there any kindliness or humour in his glance. His was now the bronzed and emotionless countenance of the sworn man-hunter, tight of lip and square of chin.

Sara's form went tense against him. She stared with eyes dilated.

"Red!"

His glance went past her unseeing. Turning, he strode toward the door.

"Red! *Red!*" she cried wildly, clutching at his arm. "Where are you going?"

"Going?" he shook her off with a bleak laugh. "I'm goin' to get the black-hearted skunk that's makin' a buzzard's paradise of this country. That's where I'm goin'."

"Red—*Wait!*"

But he was gone.


## Chapter XV

### TURKEY TALK


HOT anger raged in the sheriff's heart as he left the house. Anger at this scurvy trick played him by a fickle Fate. No longer was he pulled between two courses; no longer could he disregard his duty. He had sworn to uphold the Law and to punish evil-doers. If hard, his path lay no less plain.

And it *was* hard, damnably, bitterly hard. But no alternative was left him. As Reede only this afternoon had said "The crazy coot's gone batty! He's tryin' to kill us all!"

But now the killing spree was over if he—Red Lawler—had anything to say about it!

Whipping the gelding's reins from the veranda post, he flung himself into the saddle. At a fast run they pounded from the yard, dust rising balloon-like in their wake.

But hardly a mile had they travelled when Lawler beheld a vague horseman riding toward them. The unknown was riding leisurely, sitting straight up in the saddle, elbows flapping at either side.

Lawler pulled up and waited as a hail came down the wind. When the oncoming horseman drew close the sheriff recognised him with a snort of disgust. It was the coroner, Obe Kringle.

"Now what in seven devils does *he* want?" Lawler muttered impatiently.

He was not long in finding out.

Pulling in his horse beside that of the sheriff, Kringle halted. By the moonlight Lawler saw that there was a sly smile on the coroner's unprepossessing countenance.

"Well, well! Takin' a ride, Mr. Lawler?"

"I got no time for foolish questions," Lawler scowled. "If you got somethin' to say, then say it. If you ain't, then get outa my way. I'm in a hurry. There's been another killin'—mebbe two."

The news seemed to please the coroner for he grinned. "That's awful, Lawler—awful. I don't know what this county's comin' to. I guess you've heard Link Holladay busted loose? Remember, I warned you to put on a extra guard. If there's been two more murders you're responsible for 'em. I told you Link's friends would spring him."

"How'd he get out?"

"No one seems to know," Kringle grinned maliciously. "Quite a mystery, 'cordin' to what I've heard——"

"I guess you know as much about it as the next!" snapped Lawler, angrily.

"Are you aimin' to insinuate——?"

"If the boot fits—pull it on!"

Obe Kringle stared. But he made no move to fetch his gun. He knew better than to try a thing like that with Lawler. The sheriff was reputed to be "some fast."

"You're ridin' for a fall!" Kringle snarled vindictively.

"Don't try to act tough, Obe. You ain't big enough to cut the mustard."

"Ain't, eh? Well," sneered Kringle, "you won't be singin' so high yoreself in about two minutes. Trouble is with you, Lawler, you're all lather an' no action. You do a heap of talkin' but that's far as it ever gets. I'm bettin' you ain't got a notion now who's pullin' these killin's——"

"You're bettin' wrong then," Lawler cut in, holding his temper with an effort. "I'm on my way to nab that killer now."

Obe Kringle's jaw dropped. "Who is he?"

"I'm not sayin'. You'll find out quick enough when I bring 'im in."

A jeering laugh left the coroner's mouth. "Wind! I'm the only one round here who's got a notion who this murderin' polecat really is—an' it ain't Link Holladay!"

"Well?"

"It's that secretive, bushy-browed, bed-slat Tawson—the skunk that's been posin' as a U.S. Marshal!"

Lawler leaned forward in his saddle. "You interest me strangely. Thought you'd picked Link Holladay for the killer?"

"Not me! I was just usin' Link for a smoke screen so's I could lull Tawson into gettin' careless. Cripes, if you had half the brains I've got you'd have known all along it wasn't that cow-stealin' Holladay. I knew right from the start it was Tawson."

Lawler eyed the coroner silently. Kringle added "But knowin' it won't do you any good now."

Lawler stiffened as from far away the wind brought a vague sound of drumming hoofs. He scanned the moonlit terrain but saw no sign of the horseman. He turned to the coroner grimly.

"Just what was the meanin' of that last remark?"

"This—fella! The worthy citizens of Pecos have elected me a committee of one to ask for your resignation. You can hand over that star right now."

"Like hell!"

Lawler's right hand lashed out with unexpected suddenness. The fingers of that hand were balled into a rock-hard fist that caught Obe Kringle behind the left ear and shook him from his saddle with a wicked force. The coroner struck the sand all spraddled out.

Glaring down at him Lawler growled:

"When the Board of County Supervisors ask me for my star they can have it. Until that time it stays right here on my vest. Tell that to Pecos' worthy citizens when you get back to town!"

And, without further dallying, the sheriff slapped in his spurs and rode away.


*Chapter XVI*


## THE MAN IN THE DOORWAY


As Red Lawler rode through the starry night, the rush and slap of the gusty wind beat incessantly against his face and chest, plastering the clothes to his body and slowing the gelding's speed in no uncertain manner.

He found himself not only recalling but actually thinking of those vague-pounding hoofbeats he had heard while palavering with Kringle. What did they mean? Who was the unseen rider? Or were there two?

Soon however the futility of such speculations caused him to swerve his thoughts to the man who had escaped from the Pecos jail.

When had he gotten free? Lawler recognised that this was an important question.

Link Holladay, as he well knew, was no man's fool. Thus far he had carried on his cattle-stealing operations without having once been apprehended. The closest call the rustler had had, was the time when Lawler himself had come upon the scene just as Holladay's helpers had been about to make off with a small herd. At sight of the sheriff, the miscreants had cut loose of the stolen critters and made their getaway in safety.

Lawler did not, however, think that a man as slick as Holladay had shown himself would linger long in this vicinity when it was so palpably evident that someone was doing his best to frame him for the series of murders that were being perpetrated. To the young sheriff of Reeves County, it seemed a pretty safe bet that by this time Link Holladay would be pounding a streak of dust in the shortest cut to the Mexican border.

So thinking, he dismissed the rustler from his mind, content to let the fellow go.

He grinned faintly to himself as he recalled how he had sent the sneering coroner sprawling headlong in the sand. Perhaps the spill would teach the fellow to keep his long nose out of other folk's business. Lawler hoped so.

With an abruptness that set his nerves a-quivering the sound of a shot tore a hole through the night as Lawler crested a ridge. It came from somewhere to the left and slightly up-wind. At the same instant the big roan gelding staggered, shivered through every fibre and reared as though to take a mighty forward leap. But the leap was never taken. Instead the gelding crumpled in mid-air. Lawler felt the gallant animal that had carried him successfully through many a tight scrape go to pieces under his saddle.

With a single, smooth, lightning-quick movement the sheriff kicked his feet free of the stirrups and slid from the saddle as his horse crashed down and lay kicking spasmodically beside the trail. Dropping swiftly behind the dying animal Lawler put a period to its agony with a well-directed shot.

Red-haired anger mounted to the sheriff's brain. Some —— bushwhacking son had killed his favourite mount! All thought of caution was momentarily blotted from his mind as up he sprang, pistol in hand, and ran zig-zagging forward, his spur-rowels clacking out a warning whir.

A streak of flame blazed against the blue-black mark of a mesquite clump. Lawler ducked but kept up his zig-zag charge. The unseen's lead bit past him with the sound of angry wasps. A bullet slapped the brim of his hat; a second tugged at his sleeve as he stormed across the moonlit open.

From off to the right a second gun hurled flame-wreathed lead; a third from dead ahead. Realisation of his danger took the sheriff by the throat. He dropped flat against the earth.

Momentarily a running figure appeared sky-lighted acrest the ridge. Lawler's heavy Colt kicked back. The figure reeled and fell from view.

A rocking, roaring world of sound filled Lawler's ears; his pulses raced to the thrill of open combat. A bullet spattered

84

sand beside him. Another ripped the heel from his right boot. Gunpowder's acrid stench tore at his nostrils. For fast red moments all was turmoil and confusion. Snarls and curses resounded from the brush. Wild yells and choking screams. And over all the whine and smack of flying lead.

Then suddenly the roaring chaos of sound fell away, melting in the swift diminishing beat of fleeing hoofs and the sheriff found himself alone. Alone and horseless, a good three miles from Tranton's.

Getting himself afoot Lawler crossed to his dead gelding and removed his rifle from the scabbard thrust beneath the saddle skirts. For the moment the saddle must be left where it was. He was in a hurry and felt no desire for a three-mile walk cumbered by such a weight.

Breaking the heel from his left boot that his gait might be more even, Lawler struck out for the Box Bar T, knowing it to be the nearest place at which he could procure another mount. Seemed like everything was breaking wrong for him! Plainly this was to be a night he would long remember.

Who could have been responsible for that ornery ambush he had ridden into? Kringle? It did not seem likely for he had left the coroner spreadeagled in the sand not half an hour ago. It hardly seemed plausible that Kringle could have rounded up any partisans in such brief time and cut in ahead of the sheriff swiftly enough to have laid that ambush.

Nor did it seem to Lawler that the man responsible for that ambuscade could be the killer who signed an ironic "Justice" to his notes. For, as Lawler looked at it, the killer always worked alone.

That left but a single good alternative in the sheriff's mind. Link Holladay!

The more he thought about the rustler, the more firmly Lawler became convinced that it was indeed Link and his men who had laid that unsuccessful trap. It had, he told himself, all the earmarks of the rustler's methods. Swift attack and flight had ever been Holladay's way. He seemed to be a firm believer in the old adage that "He who fights and runs away will live to fight another day."

Evidently Holladay was too anxious to pay off his grudges to leave the country yet awhile. Likely enough, Lawler reasoned, his next step would be directed against Obe Kringle. Still one could never be certain where a man like Link was concerned. Cunning he undoubtedly was, but his vindictive nature made his probable course of action a difficult thing to gauge.

The sheriff found it no pleasure to tramp the rough miles back to the Box Bar T, and by the time he came again in sight of Tranton's ranch Lawler's hair-trigger temper was fast coming to a boil.

Recalling that Sara had said that she would likely go to bed as soon as he left, he was not surprised upon returning to see no lights in evidence.

No sense disturbing her, he reflected. He would go to the corral and rope him out a bronc and soon be on his way once more. Seemed likely he might find an extra saddle in the stable. With this thought in mind, he bent his weary steps in that direction.

Inside the building it was black as pitch and in the atmosphere there was a smell of hay. There was another smell, too—the rank smell of damp horsehide, and the lesser odours of dust and leather.

Lawler got a match from his hatband and struck it. Crimson it burst against the hovering blackness that filled the stable. It showed a drooping horse on spraddled legs, its sides slashed cruelly from the many bites of driven spurs. Still as rock the animal stood save for its heaving flanks, its head hung listless between its legs. Blood and sweat trickled from its sides.

The match in Lawler's hand went out, but not before he had seen a saddle hanging from a peg driven deep in a nearby post. Lifting it down he left the stable at an awkward run.

Dropping the saddle to the ground outside the pole corral, he removed its coil of rope and shook out a loop. Carefully he slipped inside the enclosure, closing the gate behind him. It shut with a grating squeak that put his caution to naught. The horses circled, milled at the corral's far side.

"Lost so much time now, I might's well stop an' see Sara again before I leave," he thought as softly he stalked the horses.

The twirling loop abruptly left his hand, but the horse it was aimed at ducked and the rope slid harmlessly past. The horses circled, milled again and stood watching the sheriff warily as he edged toward them building another loop.

Again the rope snaked forward. This time the long-legged bay the sheriff was after ducked too slow and Lawler hauled him in. He led the captured horse from the pen and shut the gate.

The borrowed saddle loudly smacked the back of the borrowed bay. Another ten seconds and the sheriff's Levis smacked the saddle. In no time he was dismounting before the ranch house veranda. Tethering the bay to a post he strode to the door, his spurs rasping loudly across the squeaking floorboards.

Having knocked, he stood back and built himself a cigarette while waiting for Sara's coming.

She did not come at once, so after lighting his quirly he knocked again. Inhaling deeply he felt his raw nerves soothing to the fragrant draught. "What's keepin' her?" he wondered. He could hear no kind of movement inside the house.

Slowly he grew aware of something menacing, something sinister about this stillness. A vague uneasiness gripped him. He thought suddenly of the ruined horse inside the stable. The horse recalled to his mind the drumming beat of hoofs he had heard while talking with Obe Kringle. Was that the answer to this uncanny silence?

"Lord!" he muttered, and knocked again, louder. Only echoes replied. A tingling thrill swept up the sheriff's spine. With sudden decision he grasped the knob. He pushed the door abruptly open. . . .

Gasping and groaning, Pony George's squinty eyes came blinking open. He stared in astonishment at what he saw. Twelve feet before him was a broad, flat expanse of glaring white.

"Suff'rin' snakes!" he gasped, "where be I? That there's the dangest lookin' sky ever I see in all m' borned days!"

He struggled hazily to an elbow; more hazily and with far greater alacrity he slumped back to his former position, which some time later he realised was flat on his back. It was not a comfortable position, but it did have the advantage of being stationary. And that was something!

His head ached as though some monstrous giant were beating it with the world's largest hammer. He could not understand it. What had he ever done to deserve such treatment? Where in hell was he, anyway?

He could see no flames; there was no smell of sulphur or brimstone in the air. Thus he judged he had not as yet entered the Devil's jurisdiction. That, he thought vaguely, was at least something to feel thankful for.

He glanced about him out of the corners of his eyes. He dared not move his aching head again for fear the world would spin around as crazily as it had when he'd struggled to his elbow. A wall rose up beside him on the right—a wall with a queer box-like contraption protruding from it from which dangled a funny-looking black thing on a cord.

Suddenly he realised that he was on his back and that the glaring white expanse before him was a whitewashed ceiling. Realization of his surroundings came flooding back. "My Gawd!" he exclaimed in startled conviction. "Reede's Lazy R! Who the hell brung me out here?"

Somehow he got himself afoot. He leaned groggily against the wall until his dizziness lessened to some extent. He put a hand to his aching head and it came away covered with blood. His eyes grew horror-stricken as he goggled at the crimson smearing his hand.

"I'm shot!" he howled, and likely would have swooned if he had not been so scared. His rolling eyes took in the queer box-like thing against the wall. Telephone! His glance lit on the dangling receiver that was banging against his leg and remembrance of the dire happenings presaging his present plight came swarming back. Grabbing the cord he scooped the receiver to his ear, dropping it disgustedly when he found the line was dead.

"Gosh!" as a new thought struck him, "what if that killin' fool's still lurkin' around here someplace? Cripes! George Kasta," he upbraided himself solemnly, "what the hell yuh waitin' on? If yuh got haff the sense yuh was borned with, yuh'll drag yore picket pin an' drift! An' what I mean is *now!*"

He peered about the floor seeking the envelope and letter he had dropped when the sound of that first shot had rung through the house and something hot had stung his head above the ear and shown him countless constellations he had never guessed existed. He found the papers presently and snatched them eagerly up. Red Lawler would want these! He looked again at the blurred signature initial.

"Well, mebbe it ain't a T," he muttered, holding the paper nearer to his squinted eyes. "It *might* be a J." He scowled but presently shrugged. "Anyhow I'm bettin' it's a T an' stands for Tawson. The dirty polecat! An' here I'd thought he hit fer home! The ornery, two-faced hound!"

Pony George decided that the double-dealing marshal must have been standing on the porch when he'd fired that murderous salvo. Certainly Pony George had neither sensed nor expected the other's reappearance until sound of that first treacherous shot. From then on he'd been in no position to do anything about it.

He went over himself slowly, inch by cautious inch, endeavouring to ascertain the extent of his injuries. A nasty gash along his left side below the armpit and a painful crease across the scalp, seemed to be the total extent of his damages.

"Gosh," he growled, astonished. "He sure is one careless jasper! 'Magine anyone aimin' tuh murder a gent goin' off without makin' sure his lead had done the trick!" George had, of course, no knowledge of the bloody, battered spectacle he presented or he would not have wondered at the killer's seeming negligence.

His pistol was still stuffed in the waistband of his trousers, he found with satisfaction. Making sure it still was loaded, he thrust it into his open-topped holster and proceeded to bind

88

the wound in his side with strips torn from his shirt-tail. This done to his satisfaction, he wound his neckerchief about his head and gingerly donned his shabby Stetson.

"Next thing in order, before I clear outa this dang dump fer good," he announced loudly, "is tuh take a final squint around so's tuh be sure that dang' double-crossin' polecat's gone!" Of course he did not actually doubt the killer *had* cleared out or nothing would have induced him to remain a second longer on these premises. But he liked to make himself, and any possible spectators think he had been unimpressed by the danger he had undergone during the killer's visit.

So it was with a fine air of cautious nonchalance that Pony George went tip-toeing into the kitchen with the lamp in one hand and his pistol in the other. He saw no one in the kitchen.

"An' dang lucky that hellion is thet he sloped afore I come to!"

Somewhat reassured by the barrenness of the culinary department Pony George next hazarded a peep into the room where rested Reede's mortal remains. It was a most unfortunate peep. For, sticking his head around the door, he received a nasty shock.

Across the room he beheld another door and in it a crouching man who held a lamp in one hand and a ready pistol in the other. And a more villainous-looking hombre Pony George had never seen.

A dirty Stetson was pulled low across the stranger's glaring eyes which, in the flickering light, gleamed like bits of polished jet. One side of his face was a ghastly smear of blood. Sighting Pony George his twisted lips jerked open in a fearful snarl and the straggly moustache above them appeared to bristle like a lion's mane!

"Throw up them hands or I'll blast yore m-mortal tintype!" howled the quavering notes of Pony George. But the fellow's gun came up instead. "Stop, dammit! *Stop!*" he shrilled, and his gun kicked back against his palm. The loud report chased deafening echoes smashing back and forth between the walls, through which came faintly the tinkle of shattered glass.

A great hole gaped in the stranger's chest. But he neither fell nor even staggered. Great radiating lines ran out in all directions from the place of the bullet's entrance. Yet still the hombre stood there eyeing George in shocked surprise.

And then abruptly the gun sagged in the deputy's hand.

"Gawd! A blasted mirror!" Pony George sagged. weakly against the wall.

With a doleful sigh the mortified deputy roused himself at last. "If the folks in Pecos ever hears about this they'll laff me plumb outa the state o' Texas. Cripes! What a fright that fella give me! *Whew!*"

Putting the lamp down on the table in the main room, Pony George blew it out and hastily tiptoed from the house. Like a flitting shadow he moved to the rear of the stable and got his horse. Finding the animal still standing where he'd left it gave him a gorgeous feeling—gorgeous!

"This ain't no place for Ol' Man Kasta's son," he muttered nervously. "The quicker I gets back tuh town the better I'm gonna like it. Some folks might mebbe think I ort tuh go gallivantin' over to the Bar 2 an' line my sights on that Polecat Tawson—but me, I think diff'rent!"

He nodded his head emphatically as he scrambled up into the saddle. "What you need, George Kasta," he firmly told himself, "is a dang good rest! The atmosphere round this here spread is enough tuh make a bull-moose shiver! The sooner yuh gets back tuh Pecos an' barricaded in the sheriff's office, the quicker yore blasted knees is gonna stop shakin'. Hoss—giddap!"

## Chapter XVII

### WHEN THE KILLER LAUGHED

For a second Lawler paused after pushing open the front door of Tranton's ranch house. Swiftly, then, he stepped inside the darkened hall and crouched against the wall, ready to go into action at the first warning note. Among the drifting shadows the rambling old house lay silent, lay stilled with a breathless hush that sent cold chills along the sheriff's spine.

Slowly, inch by cautious inch, he made his way along the wall. He guided himself by touch alone, for the hall was black with the Stygian murk found at the bottom of a well.

Then suddenly one reaching, feeling, outstretched hand encountered the cold frame of the sitting-room door. Again Lawler stiffened against the wall, listening. Yet only the soughing of the wind among the broad-leafed foliage of the cottonwoods drifted to his ears.

With one swift bound he placed himself inside the room with his back to a solid wall. Once more he grew stiff with listening. But naught happened and, reassured, he made his way to the table, guided by the moonlight streaming in through a window. There he struck a match and lit the lamp.

Other than himself there appeared to be no one in the
90

room. But the place was full of shadows and the sense of danger which he felt did not in any degree lessen. If anything, it grew constantly stronger as though some malignant, unseen presence watched him from a hidden place with mocking eyes.

The sheriff thrust both big hands deep within his levis pockets. He eyed the room with narrowed glance. He could think of nothing which seemed to have been disturbed; all within his range of vision seemed as he had left it earlier in the evening.

Picking up the lamp he made his way about the room, probing its shadowed corners. There was something wrong. Of this he was certain, for a sense of deep foreboding lay heavy in this house.

Lamp in hand he left the sitting-room on a tour of inspection. Despite his muscular weight he moved almost silently down the hall, his alert eyes wary.

He looked into the kitchen but found nothing out of order. No sign of an alien presence was apparent. All seemed as it should be, and wrapped in a slumbrous quiet.

He looked in the captain's bedroom, but there too everything appeared shipshape. The room was half timber, half adobe, having been added to the house ten years or so ago when the Captain had taken possession. It was cool and plainly furnished. Thick Navajo rugs were on the floor, there were two Remington lithographs on the walls and curtains at the deep-embrasured windows. A locked desk stood in one corner.

Lawler sent a final glance around and returned to the hall. His lamp cast reflections on the polished Mexican cedar of its walls and its reflections kept pace with him as he strode along. Before the door to Sara's room he hesitated. It seemed almost sacrilege to profane such hallowed spot with his uninvited presence.

What if he had guessed wrong? Supposing this crazy conviction that filled his mind were——

"Hell!" was his bitter oath. "I've got to make sure!"

Turning the knob he flung the door wide. The light of his lamp streamed in across the threshold in a yellow flood.

On that threshold he paused; stood stock-still while a tide of fear gripped up. His eyes bulged; beneath its heavy bronze his face went pale. With an effort he placed his lamp upon a dresser.

God knew his suspicions had been only too correct! No need now to see the answer to that telegram he'd sent by Pony George! No need for further guessing, worrying, or hopes.

In that endless moment that he stood there by the door

he seemed weighed down by countless centuries of despair. His last vain hope was gone, his worries and suspicions proved well founded.

Now he held the answer to .the question of why Captain Dan had been shot at; why Sara had broken their engagement; why the second bullet fired at Captain Dan had not been found. He saw now why the bushwacking killer signed his taunting notes with the word "Justice" and why the murders themselves had been committed; saw, too, why certain of the girl's explanations of the circumstances surrounding that shooting last night had not agreed precisely with the explanation given by Captain Dan.

He was satisfied beyond the possibility of a doubt he knew the killer's identity, and his soul was filled with dread.

Inside Sara's room a small table by the bed was overturned, one leg broken off with every evidence of violence. The fragments of a shattered lamp lay near the door and there was a reek of coal-oil in the air. On the farther wall a picture .hung lop-sided, its glass a mass of splinters. On the floor the worn rug was rumpled as though by scuffling feet. The girl herself was gone.

*The murderer had been back!*

There was a red neckerchief on the scuffled rug. It was Tranton's and it held the appearance of having been jerked forcibly from his neck. There were bullet holes in it and the searing mark of powder showed about the rents. And something sparkled on the floor nearby.

Lawler recognized it for what it was; a bit of braid—gold braid from the fancy vest of Tawson. Buck Tawson, the U.S. Marshal.

Lawler swayed in the doorway—swayed like a punch-drunk pugilist.

What a fool he'd been! He should have investigated his suspicions sooner! Should have waited in his office for the answer to the telegram he'd given Pony George to send! He'd been acting like a knot-head! And all because he'd been afraid to believe his astounding suspicions correct—because he had not wanted them to prove correct!

But they had been all along. He knew it now.

He bent above the lamp and blew it out. Straightening he turned and went lurching from the room and groped his way down the murky stone-flagged hall, where his spurs rang loudly, and out across the dark veranda. The moonlight struck across his face and showed it harsh with anger as he jerked the bay's reins from about the post.

It was late, damned late—but not too late to do his duty: not yet too late to vindicate the oath he'd sworn when taking office. He would go to Tawson's pronto! He would see that the Pecos Killer paid!

The long-legged bay was travelling at a dead run when Lawler settled in the saddle, his face a grim-lipped mask.

The bay's blurred hoofs beat like a drum through the moonlight night. Twisting, treacherous trails lay between its rolling muscles and the Bar 2 ranch, yet its rider drove a breakneck pace in an effort to outdistance his own black thoughts. Again and again in that nightmare ride a three-word phrase rang through Lawler's brain in letters of brass: *"Killers must pay!"*

He raked the bay's flanks with his bloody spurs but the hated phrase rang like a trumpet through the madness of his mind and would not hush. Speed could not retard it; not even the rush of his pony's hoofs could drown those bitter words.

On they raced, while beneath them the blurry miles slid by in a smeary haze of light and shadow.

They must reach the Bar 2 ere the killer fled, for it seemed plain to Lawler that the sender of these "Justice" notes was planning to leave the country just as fast as a horse could take him. And only a horse could hope to carry him beyond reach of the Law's long arm. He must reach the badlands, must lose himself and the girl in the maze of canyons, draws, ravines and gulches that cut the country to the south and west, for that way lay Mexico—Mexico and safety.

The big bay's smooth-rolling muscles between Lawler's legs made a comfortable feeling; brought to the sheriff a sense of conviction that the end of this ride would see the end of the trail.

The moon slid lower above his head, yet continued to dim the twinkling stars with its radiant splendour. Lawler rode now with loose-held rein, giving the bay a chance to choose its gait and opportunity to pick its footing. A coyote's wail came yammering across the wind that beat at his face with gusty fury and plastered his clothes tight against him in front and billowed them out behind.

The bay turned down a shallow gulch that loomed in the moonlight a natural corridor. The pony crossed its length, and up and out on the open range with never a faltering stride.

Lawler's thoughts turned to the bushwacking killer he hoped to catch ere morning came. Long since he had figured the man for Rowdy Joe Raine, one-time leader of the notorious Toyah Lake gang. Evidently, Lawler thought, the fellow's men had at last tracked their absconding leader to his lair. They had trailed him for a split or vengeance. Yet all they'd got was death.

And those "Justice" notes! Red Lawler laughed. How slick it had been of the wily Raine to make it seem that he, *the killer*, was the sufferer; that *he* was the man on vengeance bent! *Justice!* What grim mockery that signature was!

But Rowdy Joe's race was nearly run. Distasteful as the task might be, Red Lawler was fully determined to make the killer pay the price of murder.

Around a curve went the hard-running bay, and down a long straight slope. Ahead lay a bit of desert country—sand and sage and greasewood, prickly-pear and cholla. A dun, dreary expanse that glowed and shimmered in the light of the argent moon.

The sheriff crossed a casual arroyo, the bay's fast pace never faltering. Trees with twisted branches and scrubby trunks thickened along a ridgeside that soon was left in their dusty wake. The stillness of the night held awe, solemnity, and only the bay's drumming hoofs made sound.

Hards Pass Draw lay ahead.

Before them now the trail dropped dizzily to a deep ravine. Down there in the darkness grew blighted, stunted trees. Beneath their murky shadows flowed the gurgling yellow waters of Toyah Creek.

Straight down the precipitous slope Lawler drove the plunging bay. Down into the hollow and across the gurgling creek and on into the murky shadows beneath the grotesque trees where the night lay black.

A streak of crimson slashed the murk. A sharp report beat the wind apart and sent its crashing echoes back against the slope. The bay went down in a headlong fall.

When the echoes faded the thunder of hoofs was stilled. For a time the gurgling waters of the Creek made all the sound in the deathly hush. Then, sheering through the splash of unseen waters, rang a mocking laugh and the soul-torn sob of a frightened girl.


*Chapter XVIII*

## A SITUATION SQUARELY FACED

WARM rays of the morning sun falling aslant his face as they slid over the ravine's eastern wall must finally have awakened Lawler. For long minutes his aching head was in a whirl and his intellect seemed dazed and dormant. He could comprehend neither where he was nor how he came to be here. Objects seemed strangely distorted when he turned his bloodshot eyes upon them. He seemed to have a double sight. He could see two separate groves of trees; two separate gurgling creeks. But presently this handicap passed and his vision grew somewhat clearer.

With an effort he turned his head. A dead horse—a long-legged bay—lay beside the trail in a grotesque heap.

Sight of the animal brought a sudden rush of memories. Fearful thoughts engendered by his illuminating return of memory served to rouse him from his stupor. He had been hurled from his horse when the bay took the bullet that had been meant for its rider. He realized that his head must have contacted something hard. Raising an exploring hand he discovered a lump on his scalp and a large patch of hair matted and rough with dried blood.

He saw his hat beside a rock and shivered. Only that hat could have saved his life. It seemed a miracle—but perhaps he had not struck· the stone. He could recall the burst of light in his brain and a flash of terrific pain. His exploring hand touched again the ragged wound. "Couldn't 'a' been much closer, I reckon," he muttered, eyeing the flat-topped rock.

He recalled now that streak of flame among the trees and the crash of the shot. Then· his eyes fell upon a patch of sunlight and he groaned. He'd been unconscious several hours! It must be early morning now—the killer would be far away in the maze of badlands to the south.

A damnable thought, yet Lawler did not see· how he could do anything about it now. Certainly he had not hankered to have the killer shoot his horse from under him and bash his head against a rock!

Thought of the killer getting away with Sara Tranton brought new strength surging through the sheriff's veins. His head was clearing fast. Instinctively he began to seek the extent of his damage. Aside from the jagged, swollen wound in his scalp, a bruised shoulder and several minor lacerations due to his spill, he found that he was not badly hurt.

He got to his feet and stood swaying dizzily for several moments. Then his head cleared. He looked around then returned his glance to a brooding contemplation of the bay —his borrowed horse. It would be no deader.

"I'm gettin' to be hard on horses," he muttered gloomily. "Expect I'm due for some more shanks' marein' 'f I aim to get outa here."

It was then he became aware that his holster was empty. He searched the nearby brush but did not find the weapon. "Looks like I've got to start after that killer with neither a horse *nor* a gun! Reckon Obe Kringle was right at that. I'm sure one hell of a sheriff, an' no mistake!"

He approached the dead bay to see if his rifle were worth salvaging. It was not. The bay had fallen on its left side and the rifle, having been in the saddle scabbard, was smashed beyond possibility of repair.

Lawler shook his head morosely. Picking up his hat he put it on carefully so as not to reopen the wound in his scalp, and then set off slowly down the trail. He waded the creek which was quite shallow at this point and, passing up the opposite slope, got out of the ravine.

It was half a mile to Tawson's Bar 2, which lay in plain sight and looked to be about a stone's throw away. He could see no sign of anyone moving about the buildings as he struck out for them with long strides. The early morning air was cool and invigorating, yet he well knew that in less than an hour this semi-arid stretch of country would be blistering hot. He was glad he'd knocked the heel from his left boot after that rifle bullet had torn the one from his right. He dreaded to think of having to walk this distance in high heels.

Approaching the headquarters of Bar 2, Lawler circled the buildings warily. But he saw no sign of human presence, which might or might not mean anything. He *did* manage to get behind the stable without, he sincerely hoped, having been seen.

Shoving up a window he pulled himself inside. Tawson's horses were not in sight. Believing there was no longer any need for caution he passed quickly through the stable and out through the open front doors. There he received a shock, for the corral was in his vision. Inside the pole enclosure stood a dejected-looking pair of broncs. Lather-like sweat had dried on their hides. Lawler saw marks of the saddles which had been hurriedly stripped from their backs at no far distant date.

"Hell—those ain't Tawson's nags!" he exclaimed hoarsely. "Those broncs belong to Captain Dan and——" he broke off with a second oath and went sprinting toward the ranch house. A lamp was burning in the window.

He reached the porch and dashed across it, threw the front door wide and stopped. Once more he had arrived too late!

Face-down beneath the window Tawson sprawled. A dark smear between his motionless shoulders told the story. With crushing impact it came to Lawler that his hours of unconsciousness in the dark ravine had cost the marshal's life.

Tawson's pockets showed inside out. The drawers of the dresser in the far corner of the room lay upon the floor, their contents scattered round about. The killer had been after something beside the marshal's life. Had he found it?

96

Lawler thought it likely, if the sought-for thing had been here.

Spying the phone-box above the dead officer's bunk, he jerked the receiver from the hook and raised it to his ear. The line had not been cut, attesting to frantic hurry on the killer's part. Lawler called the telegraph office in Pecos.

Positive he knew the killer's identity, Lawler could not but hope that he was wrong. This call, he felt, would definitely discredit his suspicions or confirm them beyond all doubt.

Holding his lips pressed close to the mouthpiece he spoke slowly, distinctly, explaining to the operator that he was Sheriff Lawler. As proof of the fact he mentioned that yesterday afternoon he had sent off a message by Pony George to which he was expecting an answer. Would the operator kindly read said answer?

The operator would not. "You're not identified as Lawler yet," he gruffed. "Who was your wire sent to? What did it say? . . . Yeah—word for word!"

Lawler gave the desired information. A red mist floated before his vision as, satisfied, the operator quoted:

" 'Man described undoubtedly Rowdy Joe Raine, former leader Toyah Lake Gang. When last in operation Raine's hair was black, not white. So far as we know them, all other points tally.' "

Mechanically Lawler hung the receiver back upon its hook. The last remaining vestige of hope was drained from him. His suspicions had proved well-founded indeed—too damned accurate by far!

Naught but dread, despair and duty lay before him. Dread of the future; despair of the mocking horde of lonely hours stretching without end down the lane of future life— cold dark clutching dread of the duty that must be his.

He was convinced at last that Dan Tranton, self-styled "sea-dog," was the infamous Pecos Killer!

Before Lawler had been placed a vast jigsaw puzzle of murder, mystery and sudden death for solving. And now he had it solved. Each last piece slipped neatly into place to reveal an all-but-perfect picture when Captain Dan Tranton was cast in the killer rôle. There were a few loose ends but Lawler reflected morosely that when those ends were tied the picture would be perfect.

Tranton had tried to persuade him, through the unwitting employment of Sara, that someone had tried to take his life two nights ago by hurling lead through the window of his illuminated office. As further proof the Captain had offered, reluctantly, the wound in his side—which had certainly been made by a bullet. That wound, Lawler now believed, was self-inflicted by the cunning Captain in the hope that wool would be drawn across the eyes of Lawler and any other lawmen who might become interested. That wound was to help the sheriff come to the natural conclusion that Tranton was one of the men marked by the killer for death. Under such an hypothesis it would be assumed impossible that Captain Dan was himself the murderer.

Slick, thought Lawler grimly; cunning and adroit. Quite worthy of the fertile twisted brain of Rowdy Joe, the pseudonym under which Tranton had led the renegades of Toyah Lake.

This explained the mystery of the missing bullet. The second shot was the one whose bullet had torn that splintered hole in Tranton's desk, described by him as the first shot—the one with which he had been wounded. The *first* shot was the one with which the scheming Captain had, upon the ridge-top, inflicted the wound in his side which was to establish for himself an airtight alibi.

He had carefully, Lawler figured, swathed the muzzle of his pistol in his neckerchief so no powder-marks would show about the wound. Last night he had left that bullet-ridden handkerchief blood-stained on the floor of Sara's room to make it appear that in defence of his daughter he had been killed, and his body hidden someplace about the house by the murderer who later had forced Sara to accompany him in his flight. Thus Tranton had again knocked down two birds with a single stone, and had at the same time furthered the illusion that he could not possibly be himself the infamous Pecos killer.

After inflicting his wound, two nights ago, on the ridge behind the house, Tranton had fired his second shot through the office window in such a manner that it struck his desk at the appropriate angle; had then sprinted to the window, climbed through it into his office barely in time to jerk the window down as Sara pounded on his door. Thus he had proved himself within his office while the shooting outside was going on.

The running footsteps Sara claimed to have heard moving toward the house were the footsteps of the Captain making that hurried return from the ridge. He, in turn, had described those footsteps as "horse's hoofbeats" and had said they were moving *away* from the house. This must have been what originally had shown Sara that her father definitely was up to something which he did not want found out. This lying explanation must have aroused Sara's suspicions to a fever heat and forced her, in his defence, to break her engagement.

Lawler mopped his brow. His expression was dark and scowling as he sat there summing up on Tawson's bunk. His big hands were clenched and knotted at his sides.

Two nights ago, at eight-thirty, it had not been quite dark.

Leastways, it had not been so dark but what Sara *might* have seen some part of the Captain's strange performance. If she had seen such a part, it was Lawler's surmise she could have guessed the rest with reasonable accuracy and so have known her father as the killer. *That* certainly would have explained their broken engagement!

Lawler recalled that no one in Pecos or its vicinity knew for fact one blessed thing concerning the Captain's past. They did not *know* that he was or ever *had* been a captain. Though they had accepted his word for it, he had never offered proof, other than the very briny slang he seemed to sling about with ease. And if he had committed blunders in the use of sea-goingese, who had there been to point such blunders out?

Yes, Lawler admitted to himself, Dan Tranton was a slick customer from 'way back! Five years after bringing about the break-up of his gang of stage and bank robbers, Tranton had come with his gangling ten-year-old daughter to Pecos, centre of the zone of his former crimes, and here had brazenly settled down to the diverting business of putting beef on steers!

One had to admire the man's ingenuity and nerve—these, Lawler told himself, and the love Tranton apparently bore his daughter were the only things about him which an honest man could admire.

And right now Lawler was thinking that the pseudo-captain's apparent love for his motherless girl was just that —*apparent*. Could any father who really loved his daughter force that daughter to share with him the hardships and hazards of a life on the Owl-Hoot Trail?

She had kept her suspicions of him to herself out of loyalty —had made herself an accessory after the facts of Tranton's murders. That had been the meaning, Lawler reflected, of her talk last night about loyalty and duty. She had, in round-about way, sought Lawler's advice upon the subject. And he —blind fool—had as much as told her that in a man's eyes loyalty and duty were of prime importance!

He swore whole-heartedly, blaming himself that he had not at that moment really begun to suspect the Captain. He should, he bitterly thought, have suspected the suave old scoundrel from the first!—from the very moment when his explanation of the shots and footsteps had differed from the girl's!

Now Lawler saw the meaning of the single initial signed to the note Pony George had found at Reede's. That "T" had stood, not for Tawson, but for Tranton. Reede must have been the second man to have discovered the Captain's true identity, and have been offered hush money to seal his lips.

99

To seal them until such time as Tranton could get around to sealing them for good!

Lawler realized now how easily that "Justice" note had come to be found by Kringle in Doak's pocket after Pony George had finished searching. Dan Tranton had been present at that searching; when it was over and the deputy had been looking elsewhere it had been child's play for Tranton to get the note into the dead man's clothes.

Now the reason for Sara's determined defence of Link Holladay was explained. Lawler now understood that at that time Sara must have known that her father was the killer and that palpably Holladay could have had no hand in Toreva's sudden demise.

Toreva, however, must have known all along that Tranton was the murderer of Doak. Very likely the Captain had given the Mexican his split long ago, so had nothing to fear from him. Then, perhaps, after Doak's killing Toreva had demanded hush money. If so, Toreva had made a fatal mistake in psychology.

Lawler's thoughts next turned to the man who lay so still upon the floor. Tawson had undoubtedly been recognized by Tranton for what he was—a U.S. Marshal. Tawson was in the country to get him: Tranton had simply beaten the marshal to the jump. Having planted the bit of braid in Sara's room last night to implicate Tawson, the Captain evidently had later found reason to close the marshal's lips for good with one quick stroke of a knife.

Perhaps he had hoped that the authorities, investigating the marshal's death, would become inextricably tangled in a web of close-spun suspicion when knowledge of that bit of braid in Sara's room, together with the bloody, bullet-pierced neckerchief of the girl's father, came to their attention.

He had been pretty certain, at any rate, should the Law ever stumble on a correct interpretation of events he would by that time be safely beyond its reach.

A far worse thought abruptly burst on Lawler's consciousness: Tranton, now, would never dare turn Sara loose—he must keep her with him constantly or seal her mouth forever! For free, Sara would place him in the shadow of the noose!

Lawler wiped cold perspiration from his forehead. Tranton had plotted well, had covered his tracks with consummate skill. He would have been caught red-handed last night but for his infinite care of detail. Tranton had known the sheriff for a man of dogged tenacity and stubborn determination and had left nothing to chance. He had expected Lawler to follow him and had awaited him in the spot of greatest vantage along the trail he was sure Lawler would be taking. Crossing the blackness of that stretch of ground beyond the creek, Lawler had been plainly silhouetted against the glowing moonlit wall behind. Only for the sudden upflinging of the bay's head, Lawler would have died—and it was patent that the killer thought he had!

Swiftly the sheriff reviewed his case against Dan Tranton. The Captain, recognizing the marshal as soon as Tawson had appeared in Pecos, to save his neck had figured upon a succession of ruthless killings. There were too many witnesses against him; he had to whittle their number down—for killing Tawson alone would do no good. Another marshal would be sent to take his place. Desperate, his hiding place at last discovered by the law as well as by members of the gang he had betrayed, Tranton had sent for Max·Smith. Then he had killed Doak, who was already on the ground. Next had come the faked attempt upon his own life, designed to turn suspicion elsewhere. This illusion he had promptly strengthened by giving out an impression that he knew the would-be assassin and was determined to keep the fellow's identity to himself.

Next in Tranton's ruthless campaign to gain for himself impregnable security had come the murder of Manuel Toreva. A bleak smile quirked the sheriff's lips as he reflected that Big-Ear Lester's testimony against Holladay, save for mention of the latter's name, would have fit the Captain equally well.

Then Smith had arrived and ridden blithely to his doom. Reede's death had followed swiftly and on the heels of that Tranton had staged the false struggle in Sara's room to plant suspicion on Tawson and lure Red Lawler to his end. That Lawler had not met his end in the dark ravine was certainly no fault of Tranton's.

And by now, he reflected darkly, Dan Tranton and the daughter he was kidnapping must be far away among the maze of draws and canyons that gouged the country to south and west.

Stepping from Tawson's shack out into the sandy yard, the sun's hot smash struck Lawler like a hammer. The near-noon air was filled with a dry heat that scorched the nostrils, that drew all moisture from his body.

For long moments, nevertheless, he stood staring out across the shimmering layers of heat that lay in stratas above the yellow earth. His gaze went out across the rolling range, the distant ranches, the sand and desolation. This was his kingdom. Nearly as far as he could see in any direction his word was law. With Tranton riding clear, and each moment taking Sara farther from him, the thought was a mockery that made him squirm with its torture.

Then his lean jaw clenched and he squared his broad shoulders with resolution. Though it be the last act he performed in life, he meant to catch Dan Tranton and make him pay.

## Chapter XIX

### "I GOT TOO MUCH RESPECT"

Pony George Kasta looked but little the worse for wear on the morning following his harrowing experiences at Joe Reede's Lazy R. He sat with his spurred heels resting comfortably on the sheriff's desk, a pad of finger-marked white paper on his knee and a stubby pencil gripped in hand.

To be sure, there was a home-made bandage about his head that peeped forth a trifle beneath his hat and aroused considerable speculation on the part of those who saw it. It had, in fact, surprised a comment from no less a personage than Obe Kringle, the coroner, when Pony George had stopped by to tell him there was a chore for him at the Lazy R. But the deputy could not be led to talk about the manner in which he had come to require the need of a bandage about his cabeza. Nor had he a great deal to say anent why Obe Kringle was needed at the ranch of Reede.

"But what in the heck do I wanta drive 'way out there for?" complained the coroner.

"Couldn't say."

"Well, what's out there?"

"Reede."

"I can see him in town without stirrin' from my porch," objected Kringle.

"Not no more, yuh can't."

"Why——"

"He's the one that's needin' yore attention."

"You don't mean to tell me Reede's dead?"

"He'll never be no deader!"

"My soul!" gasped the startled coroner.

"An' Reede's body," finished the deputy drily. "oughta make a dang good pair!"

And now here was Pony George safely ensconced in the sheriff's office inside the Pecos courthouse where he felt reasonably safe—for the moment. But though he did not believe the Pecos Killer would come seeking for him here, he was a man who believed, likewise, in taking no more chances than were absolutely necessary.

102

In the furtherance of this commendable philosophy he had placed with considerable effort a pile of tin cans, one atop the other, behind the closed office door in such a manner that they formed a hazy resemblance to the famous Leaning Tower. A person opening that door from the hall side would be bound to announce his coming, intentionally or otherwise.

Besides this ingenious alarm system, Pony George had also taken the liberty of moving Lawler's desk from its accustomed position so that, from where he now sat behind it, he commanded an unobstructed view of both windows.

"One thing that corpse an' cartridge occasion did fer me which I got tuh admit is right helpful," he muttered thoughtfully. "It sure give me some right smart ideas fer m' Ballad of Kyote Cal."

He looked pridefully down upon the four scrawled lines of writing soiling the virginity of the pad's top sheet:

> "He was tall an' slim an' quick as a cat,
> An' like a cat he walked——
> His clothes was black, an' black was his hat;
> Like honey, his voice when he talked.

"George," he complimented himself modestly, "that there verse is sure a dinger! Why, gosh—it's good as the stuff that fella Shakespeare used tuh write." Re-reading the verse he added, judicially: "In fact, I expect it's a little better."

For several moments longer he continued to regard his masterpiece with all the fond pride of a loving parent. Then once again he wet his stub of pencil on the tip of his tongue and made ready to get down to the serious business of composing another four lines.

But the Muse must needs be coaxed, he found. It was slow work, yet little by little new thoughts began to form. Word by word and phrase by phrase, with many a muttered oath and grunt, he managed to tabulate another quatrain:

> "One hand, long an' lean, clung close to his Colt;
> As he chuckled right nasty an' grim——
> "Jest lissen tuh me, yuh dirty Piute;
> That dame yuh been neckin's my bim!"

Pony George pursed his leathery lips as he scanned appraisingly his latest jingle for posterity. From the expression that began slowly to dawn on his ugly countenance it was obvious that the verse afforded him a good deal of quiet satisfaction. Forgetting for the nonce to keep a look-out for his playmate of the previous night, he tilted his hat rakishly and stroked his long nose.

103

"That ain't so bad," yet his voice was dubious. "Still—it ain't so dang good. Leastways, it ain't in the same class with that last 'un. *That* verse is sure gonna be right-down hard tuh beat, an' I ain't meanin' *if* or *perhaps!*"

He regarded the two quatrains pensively. "Now le' me see. Cal hadn't ort tuh stand fer any talk like that from a stranger. Cal's a real tough hombre—like m' boss, Red Lawler. Only Red ain't so orn'ry as Cal. Trouble with Red is he ain't got no poetry in his soul. He can't sabe it's poetry makes the world spin round!

"Hmm. Now what the hell was I thinkin' about when Red got me off the track? . . . Oh, yeah—Kyote Cal. Wal, it's plain that Cal ort tuh have some sorta comeback fer this obstreperous stranger. 'Course, Cal don't savvy what a mean jasper he's buckin' up against, so he'd be feelin' pretty mean, seems like. Le's see, now . . ."

> Cal whirled around quick, an' he sez "Looky here,
> Pilgrim, yo're headin' fer hell——
> I don't give a damn if yo're mean as a mule;
> It's time someone sounded yore knell!"

A tremendous rattling crash jerked Pony George's startled eyes to the door. It was standing wide open and, framed in the opening stood a man. George gulped uneasily, for the man was Red Lawler and Lawler's expression was not, by any stretch of his duty's ready imagination, one of amusement.

"Well, what happened to you?" Lawler gruffed, eyeing the bandage that showed from under George's hat. "That the result of them shots I heard when you called me the second time from Reede's? Looks like you been in a fight."

"Fight!" snorted Pony George, indignant. "Lemme tell yuh, Red Lawler, yuh dang nigh lost yore best depity las' night! Do yuh realize I dang near got massacreed? An' speakin' of fights—yuh don't look so durn festive yoreself."

"I ain't feelin' festive neither," Lawler's tone was curt.

"Looks like yuh been playin' tag with a mountain lion."

"Playin' hell would be more like it! George the Pecos Killer's pulled his picket pin an' sloped—with Sara Tranton."

Pony George's lower jaw dropped open; his eyes grew big and round.

"The Pecos Killer," Lawler told him, "is Dan Tranton——"

The next morning posses under the direction of Sheriff Lawler and Deputy Kasta set out from Pecos to comb the surrounding country in an effort to run to earth, dead or alive, the notorious Pecos Killer.

Aside from the forty-one men armed and outfitted by the sheriff's office, there were innumerable smaller parties unofficially scouring the vicinity in the hope of gaining some part of the seven-thousand dollar reward offered by Reeves County for the capture or death of Dan Tranton. It was a red-letter occasion in the history of Pecos.

But the man-hunters did not come up with the elusive and much-sought Captain, neither that day nor the next, nor the day after that. For two weeks hard-riding posses under the grim-lipped sheriff and his poetic deputy searched Reeves County from end to end.

They combed the desert country and all that rolling stretch of range south of Pecos to Balmorhea in ever-widening circles. But to no avail. Dan Tranton had completely vanished. Either he had made good his escape and left the country, or he had found some hole-up never previously brought to the attention of the forces of law and order.

Kringle brought his juries together and returned verdicts of murder against Tranton for the deaths of Joe Reede and Buck Tawson.

During the following two weeks the reward-hungry posses and many private citizens, all searching with the same motive, laboured mightily in a hunt that wore their leathered horses down to skin and bone.

With unwearying persistence they combed the bad-lands and mountain areas again and again. With dogged tenacity they fought the stinging grit and stifling heat of the desert country in a wallowing, wide-flung search across the shifting sands. But they did not cut sign of the wanted men, though occasionally Link Holladay and other lesser fry were seen watching them with mocking grins. Once or twice Holladay even helped, though most of his time was given over on such occasions to razzing the other searchers.

It was exasperating, the way Dan Tranton evaded their far-flung net. The search had gone from Kent almost to Angeles; from Orla to beyond the town of Sand Hills; from Sand Hills in a straight line south to a junction with the Pecos River; westward along that river to a certain spot where they swung southwest to the southwestern boundary of Reeves County, returning through Balmorhea State Park to Toyahvale, thence to Kent and back to Pecos.

On the fifteenth day Lawler gave it up and disbanded the posses.

But he did not give up his intention of bringing the killer back to face the penalty for his crimes.

"Can't see what yuh're goin' to do about it," Pony George told him cheerfully as they sat in the sheriff's office that afternoon. "Looks like tuh me we been pretty well all over this county. Yuh've warned all the surroundin' counties an' we've plastered pictures of 'im all over the whole dang estate. Reeves County has sure been raked with a fine-tooth comb."

"Yeah," Lawler hunched his broad shoulders, took a turn or two about the room, "an' it ain't done a mite of good. Tranton's still ridin' free an' easy an' Sara ain't been heard from." He thrust his hands deep-down in his pockets. Eyeing George intently, he added, "But we ain't hunted none outside the county."

Pony George squinted owlishly. "Y'ain't figgerin' tuh go clear tuh Mexico after 'im, are yuh?"

"If necessary—yeah." Lawler's tone was flat and serious. "Get it into your head, George, that I'm gonna get Dan Tranton, one way or another. It's my duty to apprehend him for these killin's. What do you think I feel like when I recall how he's forcin' Sara to stick with him through all the hardships his flight must be facin' him with?"

"What do yuh think," George countered, "Sara'll feel like when yuh bring her ol' man back tuh face a hangman's rope? Ever spent any thought on that?"

"Do you think I'm a fool?" Lawler growled.

"Why don't yuh turn yore star in then an' give it up? If yuh ain't sheriff no more, folks can't expect yuh to risk yore neck huntin' Tranton an' tryin' tuh bring 'im in."

"I'm not dodgin' the issue. I ain't the side-steppin' kind. What's more," Lawler said grimly, "To-morrow mornin' I'm headin' for points south."

"Yuh mean—Mexico?" George's eyes were round.

"I mean . . . Well, mebbe it'll be better if you don't know. But I'll say this much; I'm figurin' to go where my star'll be a damned sight more of a liability than a asset. An' I ain't aimin' to come back till I've found Tranton an' Sara— if Sara's still alive."

"Suppose she ain't?"

"Then," said Lawler darkly, "I'll be comin' back alone."

## Chapter XX

## "WHAT'S YOUR HURRY, MR. HOLLADAY?"

IN the one-room shack serving the Bar 2 for a ranch house since the advent of Buck Tawson, a group of hard-faced men were gathered about the rough plank table leisurely finishing a supper of beans, bacon and biscuits. Chief among this group was the burly Holladay—gentleman of the Hungry Loop.

Rubbing his bottle-like nose with a calloused hand that was none too clean, Holladay gave his companions a hard stare.

"To-night," he said, "I'm figgerin' to take a pasear into Pecos. I got a long chore in a dark suit what's needin' tendin' bad."

"But," began one of the men. Holladay's rough growl rode through his voice:

"Account's too long past due right now. I ain't figgerin' to wait no longer. I'm gonna make that slat-sided son of a rattlesnake's grandmother wish to hell he'd never been born!"

"Kringle, yuh're meanin', I take it?" asked one of the others thoughtfully. "Be kinda risky, won't it?"

"Risky? What of it? You ain't figgerin' that mealy-mouthed windbag could ever beat me to the draw, are yuh, Tierny?"

"Wal, look——" said Tierny soberly. "Pecos is kinda on the prod right now. Be better tuh wait. S'posin' someone should recognize yuh?"

"What if someone does? Hell, they got nothin' on me!" sneered Holladay, wiping a greasy hand on the scarred batwing chaps he wore. "I been weaned for quite some spell an' figger on bein' plumb able to take care of any little thing what comes along."

"Yuh can't lick the whole damn town!"

"Whole damn town won't try pickin' on me. Leastways, not all to oncet."

"But what'll it get yuh? Seems tuh me you are gettin'

107

kinda reckless, Link. That Kringle gent ain't worth a two-bit ante in this game. Anyways, he's the one what fixed yo' get-away."

"What's that got to do with it?" Holladay scowled. "He's the one what got me slapped in gaol in the first place, the lyin' hound! Did you ever know me tuh own a blackjack with my name burned on it?"

"Jest the same," Tierny observed quietly, "I can't see no sense in riskin' more of the same jest tuh take a whack at the fella what got yuh out."

"Look," growled Holladay viciously. "That skunk tried to frame me with the murder of Toreva. There can't no gent frame Link Holladay an' go round blowin' about it. I'm fig-gerin' to beat that coroner up so bad he'll think a Kansas twister struck him. After that, he'll mind his own business, mebbe."

"Wal," shrugged Tierny. "It's yore funeral, I reckon."

Holladay laughed. "If there's any funeral it won't be mine. I'll be back 'fore mornin' an' we'll strike out for the Bar-rillas. Keep yore eye on——"

"What yuh want us tuh do with——"

"Jest keep on like we been doin'," Holliday cut in, "an' see that yuh keep these hellions in hand."

Shoving back his chair Holladay got to his feet and went out to the corral where he roped himself a bronc, slapped a saddle on its back, slipped on a bridle and went loping off toward town.

Coroner Obe Kringle was a man who held a high opinion of himself. He knew that the best way to get ahead in a world of more or less competition was to play politics and make it a habit to grease the right palm. He had no scruples; his motto was "Every man for himself." He had done quite nicely with this system.

On this particular evening he was feeling very much at ease as he sat rocking in his comfortable adobe house on the outskirts of town. He was taking a deal of pleasure from the fact that Red Lawler and his posses had returned empty-handed this afternoon from their two-weeks' search for Dan Tranton.

"Damn young squirt!" he growled, then chuckled as he thought of the discomfiture that must be Lawler's as a re-sult of his vain efforts to apprehend the Pecos Killer.

"Won't be long now," he reflected smugly, "till the county commissioners ask for Lawler's resignation. When that wel-come time arrives, perhaps this county'll see a real gent packin' that star—Obe Kringle, mebbe." And he smirked in anticipation.

Rising presently from his easy chair by the window he crossed to the table and lit the lamp. Dusk had fallen outside and the coroner was a man who preferred much light; he had no use for shadows. He closed the door too, for the evening air was cool and invigorating and Kringle was a man who liked his ease. Oftentimes of an evening he would have a few friends in for a game of stud; Zeb Hartley, who ran the general store, and other prominent townsmen. Obe particularly enjoyed these "friendly" games as he nearly always won—due, perhaps to the fact that most of his companions played according to Mr. Hoyle while Kringle was a man who believed in making his own rules.

"Reckon I'll call Zeb up now an' see if him an' some of the others don't want to drop over for a little stud to-night," he thought. And going to the phone he called Zeb. And Zeb said they'd be glad to "set in" for a spell. Zeb promised to round up some other boys soon as he finished figuring on his accounts.

The coroner returned to the comfort of his easy chair by the window.

He must have been dozing. For he roused to the thump of steps crossing the porch. He hastened to the door and flung it open. He was expecting to see Zeb and the others, but what he *did* see gave him much the same sort of shock he would have realized had someone struck him unexpectedly across the head with a crowbar. He was almost floored, for Link Holladay stood there grinning.

"Howdy, Obe. Ain't got company, have you? Like tuh palaver some."

"I ain't got company," Kringle said, "but I'm expectin' some any minute."

Holladay forestalled his attempt to shut the door by thrusting between it and its frame a booted foot. Then pushing Kringle before him he stalked into the house and shut the door.

"Wal," he said, looking curiously around, "nice place yuh got here, Obe. You must be doin' pretty well. You givin' the killer a cut?"

"What do you want?" Kringle's tone was not quite petulant. He was beginning to wish he'd left the big rustler in gaol.

"Come tuh thank you for all yuh've done for me, Obe. Special-like fer producin' that blackjack at the inquest the other day an' claimin' yuh found it under Toreva's window. Mebbe you did find it there. But yuh never found it like it was when yuh showed it tuh that damn jury 'cause I never put my name on a blackjack in my life."

"Why—why——" Kringle stammered and fell abruptly silent.

"This here's a swell night for a murder, Obe," said Holladay pleasantly.

A hoarse cry broke from Kringle's throat as he backed away. "Wh—what you want with me?"

"Why, look, Obe—I ain't forgotten the way yuh run on me at that inquest you held on Toreva. Kinda figgered mebbe I'd swing for Toreva's death, eh? You yeller cur! I'm gonna take you apart, fella, an' throw the pieces out the window!"

Kringle could see the rustler's eyes glowing like smouldering coals beneath the downturned brim of his shabby hat. The rustler's thin lips were stretched tight across his huge buck teeth in a grimace that sent a wave of fear up the coroner's spine. A feeling of helplessness seemed to have him in its grip; the blood surging through his arteries seemed to curdle as he stared at the advancing Holladay.

A wolfish growl left the rustler's lips. There was murder in his glance.

"Gawd's sake, Link!" the coroner screamed. "I never done it, I tell yuh!"

"Him as sups with the Devil needs a damn long spoon," jeered Holladay. "You ain't got the guts for the kinda stunt you tried to pull. A single-barrel squirt like you, Obe, ain't got no business on the river side of the corral. It yuh know any prayers now's the time tuh say 'em."

Leaning forward Holladay reached out a calloused hand toward Kringle's collar.

With sudden, desperate leap Kringle avoided that outstretched hand and sent his own diving beneath his frock coat for the weapon he always carried in a spring holster beneath his arm.

"Why, you drivellin' nit!" snarled Holladay. His reaching hand dropped hipward. As it struck, a burst of flame sheared outward from his thigh.

Obe Kringle reeled against the wall, jack-knifed and slid forward on his face as the shot's concussion snuffed the lamp and sent wild echoes smashing through the dark.

Gun gripped ready Holladay whirled, flung open the door and went sprinting out across the porch making for the horse that stood with grounded reins just below the railing.

Shouts rose from a group of shadowy figures sprinting toward him from down the street. Holladay's gun whipped up; flame spurted luridly from its weaving muzzle. A man reeled screaming from the running group. A second sprawled headlong. A third clutched an arm and staggered, Shouts—curses—pandemonium!

Someone in that milling blur of figures produced a pistol

and opened up. Lead splashed the adobe at Holladay's back. Jumping the rail he landed in the saddle, thrust an arm beneath his horse's neck and gathered in the reins. Viciously his star rowels jabbed the animal's flanks. With a frightened squeal it bolted for the open range.

Three hundred yards it covered at rocket speed. Then Holladay sawed the reins back savagely, jerking his animal's head back forcibly against its chest. On braced legs the horse skidded to a stop. Broadside before it loomed the dark blur of another horseman and the town lights glinted on the carbine across his lap.

"What's your hurry, Mr. Holladay?" came Lawler's cold drawl through the gloom.

Holladay cursed bitterly. "What the hell you doin' out here?"

"Might be I was enjoyin' the evenin' breeze. Then again I might have been waitin' here for you. Take your choice."

"Some day," Holladay snarled, "I'm gonna have to gutshoot you!"

"You've certainly been takin' plenty of practice—must be your eyesight's failin', Link."

Had Holladay's pistol not been empty at that moment, he looked as though he would have shot it out with Lawler then and there. Even as it was he appeared sorely tempted to chance his luck and jerk his Winchester from the saddle. But what he did was to grunt, "Expect yuh're figgerin' to pull me in fer breakin' gaol . . . ?"

"When a rim-fire man like you breaks gaol I never let it bother me," Lawler drawled contemptuously. "Was aimin' to let you loose in the mornin' anyhow. No, I ain't after you for breakin' gaol—'f I had been I coulda grabbed you before when you was helpin' some of my men hunt Tranton."

"Then if you ain't wantin' me choke off the blat an' git outa my way!"

"Hold on a minute, Link. Seems like you might know what's all the commotion about down yonder. Seems like it might be in front of Kringle's place. Seen Obe lately?"

"What if I have?"

"Be kinda tough, say, if you'd seen him to-night an' it was found that he'd been killed," said Lawler softly. "Mebbe you an' me better ease down that way an' see what's up. Seems like I heard shootin' a spell back. Got any burnt shells in your hog-leg, Link?"

Holladay shoved his horse in close beside that of the sheriff, as though to hand his pistol over for inspection. Instead his clenched fist drove abruptly at Lawler's head. Lawler ducked, and the carbine roared. A streak of flame tore past the rustler's shoulder. Then Holladay swayed in, got his

hands about the weapon's barrel and wrested it from Law
ler's grip. Aloft he swung it, and downward in a flailing arc
at the sheriff's chest as Lawler flung himself backward over
his horse's rump. He lit rolling and, bounding to his feet,
jerked the pistol from his holster.

Holladay sank the spur as Lawler fired and missed. Lawler emptied his pistol. But Holladay stayed in the saddle and
his pounding horse soon vanished in the black of the open
range.

## Chapter XXI

### PEACEFUL INTERLUDE

By the time Lawler had caught his frightened mount he
saw no sense in trying to overtake the fleeing rustler. He
believed he had wounded Holladay, basing his opinion upon
the way Holladay had seemed to sway in the saddle. At any
rate, just now it was Lawler's business to see what had happened down the street.

So turning in that direction he jogged along till he
reached the coroner's house. There he stopped. A crowd of
angry, gesticulating townsmen before the porch fell silent
as Lawler swung from the saddle and strode through them
to the porch and up the steps and on inside.

At one side of the room Zeb Hartley and his friends stood
moveless. The light from the rekindled lamp clustered the
floor with shadows. But as Lawler approached he saw the
limp figure of a man upon the floor. It was flat upon its back
staring ceilingward with sightless eyes. Obe Kringle.

"He was on his face when we came in," explained Hartley.
"We turned him over to see was there anything we could do.
There wasn't. The fella what shot him jumped out the door
as we came runnin' up. He threw down on us. Shot Bill
Townsend deader'n hell. Nicked Zeke Loftus an' Ray Bran-
ton. He jumped to his saddle an' made a getaway. I had a
gun an' done some firin' but I don't guess I hit 'im."

"Who was he? Anyone see his face?"

No one answered. Then Hartley said, "Too dark tuh make
out his face from where we were. We oughta have more
lights down here. This end of town's dark as the inside of
Jonah's whale. I've said it afore an' I'll say it ag'in. Damn
shame! 'F it hadn't been so dark Obe might be alive this minute. Who knows?"

Another man said, "Gettin' so a fella ain't even safe in his own house no more."

Lawler made no examination of the coroner. He'd seen too many dead men before not to know when life had departed. Obe Kringle he knew had been dead some minutes. And the chances, he thought, were about one hundred to one that Link Holladay had done the killing.

But he saw no reason for telling the townsmen that.

"First thing in the mornin'," he said, "I'll get on the killer's trail. Can't see to do anything before mornin'. One of you gents can call ol' Doc Shantert in to look at the body, then you can put it on the bed."

After putting up his horse, Lawler went directly to his office. Pony George was holding down the shrieval chair.

George looked up when Lawler came in and flung his hat on the desk. "Was that shootin' I heard a while back?"

"Think mebbe it was thunder, George?"

"Wal, there ain't no call for yuh tuh get sarcastic. *I* couldn't tell from here what it was, could I?"

"I don't expect it occurred to you to get out of that chair long enough to find out, did it?"

"Wal, sufferin' snakes!" Pony George protested. "I figgered *somebody* oughta stay in this office in case there was a robbery or another murder in town an' some gent come lookin' for the law!"

Lawler sighed. "No use, I reckon," he said resignedly. "You're you an' Gawd himself, I expect, couldn't change you." After a moment of disgusted silence he told of the happening up town and of his brush with Holladay.

"That fella's bad medicine!" Pony George declared, pounding the desk with his fist for emphasis. "Somethin' oughta be done about gents like him. They give this county a bad repitation."

"Yeah," said Lawler drily and, thrusting his big hands deep into his levis pockets, fell silent, staring gloomily at the floor.

"D'yuh know what?" Pony George asked after a time. "I think that durned rustler has some kinda connection with Dan Tranton."

"It's an idea," Lawler agreed. "Considerin' its pedigree I reckon we ought to treat it kindly."

Pony George sniffed. "Anyhow," he said, "Link Holladay showed up around here just a short spell before Doak an' the rest of them jaspers." He regarded the sheriff sombrely. "Do you reckon Link was bad hit?"

"Couldn't tell. Might not have been hit at all. It was damn dark out there an' I had to do my triggerin' by guesswork mostly. Look like he clutched at the horn once but I might been mistaken. I'll give Link credit—he's crafty as a lobo. If he figgered I'd quit shootin' he'd act that way, anyhow."

Pony George nodded. "I expect you hit him. But I'm bettin' we don't find him layin' round anyplace in the mornin'. Reckon this'll sorta put a crimp in yore plans for leavin' town, won't it?"

Lawler pursed his lips thoughtfully. "No," he said at last. "Reckon I'll be leavin', anyway. You can ride along a spell an' we'll keep our eyes out for Link's carcass. 'F we find it you can pack him back to town."

"Shucks," said George. "I was sorta figgerin' tuh trail along."

"Where?"

"Why, huntin' Tranton, of course. Wherever yuh was figgerin' tuh go."

Lawler shook his head. "Be too dangerous, George. You better stay here. I gotta leave a deputy here anyhow. No tellin' what I'll bump into."

"How about appointin' Zeb Hartley's kid depity till we get back?"

Lawler looked at George in some surprise. "I can't see why you're wantin'——"

"Flip a coin," cut in the deputy, anxiously. "Heads I go, tails I stay."

"All right. If you wanta be buzzard bait," said Lawler wearily, "far be it from me to stop you. Here goes," and he flipped the coin. It landed heads.

"Now," said Pony George jubilantly, "Mr. Kasta's li'l boy gets tuh go!"

"I'm some surprised you wantin' to go this way. Thought you was puttin' in all your time on that coyote ballad?"

"I've done finished that. Can't think how to start another'n so I might's well go with you. Might be I would get some new ideas," George said hopefully.

"Finished that thing, have you?" Lawler said. "How's it end? Cal get killed?"

"Wal—ef yuh insist on knowin', I'll read 'er," said George, and dug hastily in his pocket for the pad.

"I wasn't insistin'. But if you want an opinion, I'll listen," Lawler said. Leaning back in his chair he closed his eyes. "Better read that last verse over again so I can catch on where you left off."

"Wal, sure," said George, and—

" 'Oh, yeah?' says the stranger, 'Yuh son of a Chink!
    Git yore paws up an' keep 'em right still——
    Don't gimme no sass, yuh mangy Kyote,
    'Cause it's you thet I'm pinin tuh drill!'

114

"At this orn'ry insult Kyote Cal swore,
    An' his hand to his holster did flash——
The stranger's gun spoke, an the sound of Cal's fall
    Was drowned in the thunderous crash!

"Cal uttered a sigh, an' his eyes they got dim,
    As he slumped to the sawdust-spread floor——
An' the stranger's harsh laff rang out like a blast,
    As he crouched, gun in hand, by the door.

"Swift his narrow-eyed glare flashed round like a curse,
    As he looked for Kyote Cal's dame——
She stood there by the bar, with her hand on a knife,
    An' her charms standin' out like a flame.

"All the folks in that place stood back wooden-faced,
    As the stranger cat-stepped toward our Lou——
From his lips burst an oath, an' his eyes filled with fear
    As her hand flung the knife straight an' true.

" 'Tis a saga of sorrow, a tale bold but true.
    That yuh've heard of ol' Kyote Cal——
An' the moral this saga has tried tuh drive in, is
    *'Don't be a fool fer a gal!' "*

Despite his troubles Lawler chuckled.
"How'd yuh like 'er?" Pony George anticipated praise.
"So-so," said Lawler. "Reminds me of the curate's egg."
"Was it good?"
"Yeah—in spots!"


## Chapter XXII

## "TWO FELLAS HELD THE STAGE UP"

CHILL daybreak was in the air and beneath the heavens the range lay grey and lifeless when Lawler and Pony George rose on the following morning. After a cold breakfast of beans and biscuits, wolfed down with scalding java, George went to the stable for their horses while Lawler washed the dishes.

Great scarlet streaks appeared in the eastern sky. The light grew steadily stronger and crimsoned along the far horizon as the sun got out of bed.

Old Sol's beaming face was just commencing to peep above the rim of the world when the sheriff and Pony George, rifles under their stirrup leathers, food in their saddle pockets and blankets rolled in slickers behind their cantles, struck out on the trail of Link Holladay.

The air was cold and invigorating and the breaths of horses and men shot out in smoky plumes before them though both lawmen, experienced desert men, knew that in hardly more than an hour it would be stifling hot.

"Reckon he's got a pretty good start by now," offered Pony George.

"If he was badly wounded we'll find him," said Lawler grimly, "because we won't have travelled far. Somehow, though, I kinda think mebbe he was funnin' me when he reeled in his saddle las' night. If I hit him at all it prob'ly was only a nick—mebbe caught him in the arm."

"Hope it was his gun arm, then. That jasper can shoot! Took four shots at them fellas last night; killed one an' nicked two others. That's shootin', if anyone should ride up an' ask yuh!"

"Yeah—not bad. Mighta been luck though. Somethin' tells me we ain't gonna come up with Link to-day. Let's shake it up a little. These tracks are pretty plain."

They increased their pace to an easy lope, Lawler watching the trail, Pony George keeping a nervous eye on the surrounding country. They wanted no ambushes this morning.

Trail-lure gripped them. For a time the set of hoofprints they were following, representing as it did the flight of a killer, was all-engrossing. The sun's rays grew hotter and hotter, yet they did not notice.

"This is Link's trail, all right," Lawler muttered presently. "He's ridin' that hog-back roan; I'd recognize them tracks anyplace. Two-year-old whittler."

"Reckon that's so, Red. That sign is big as soup plates." Pony George shot a sidelong glance at his superior. "Mebbe we better ease up a little."

"What for? These broncs can hold this pace all day."

"I wasn't thinkin' 'bout the nags. Looks like Link's headin' straight fer the Bar 2. What we gonna do if his gang's holed up there?"

"Do?" Lawler laughed grimly. "We're goin' in an' arrest him—that's what!"

"Yeah, but—mebbe his gang won't like it."

"Mebbe they won't. That's *their* lookout. If they wanta put up a scrap they got nobody to blame but themselves if they get hurt."

"Yeah—but these corpse an' cartridge occasions is hard on weak hearts."

"Shouldn't worry you any. Fella what smokes chewin' tobacco in his pipe hadn't oughta do any complainin' 'bout a weak heart."

George frowned and pulled the rifle from his scabbard, rode with it across his saddle. "If they's any shootin', all I hope is I get first shot!"

Talk fell away as mile by mile the sign showed fresher. The lawmen grew more alert, more cautious seldom topping rises without first spying out the land afoot. Around nine-thirty they drew close to Tawson's former shack. There was no sign of life about the place. The pole corral was empty.

"Gone!" growled Pony George, as though disappointed, and thrust his rifle back in its scabbard viciously.

"The roost sure looks a heap empty for a fact," Lawler admitted. "George, you take the south-east side an' I'll scout north-east. 'F you see fresh tracks sing out."

They parted, George reluctantly. Lawler scouted the ground to the north and west of the Bar 2 shack in a wide half circle. Abruptly Pony George let out a howl that brought him pounding up.

Four sets of hoofprints led due south. "That's them," said Lawler softly. "Look—there's the tracks of Link's roan whit-tler! He's joined his men an' they're headin' south. Prob'ly got some hide-out in the hills. Those tracks ain't more'n four hours old—five, at most. C'mon, let's go!"

They struck off along the trail at a fast lope.

"Where yuh s'pose they're aimin' fer?" yelled Pony George, after half an hour of steady riding. "Reckon they're headed fer the Injun Paintin's?"

Lawler shook his head. "Trail's gonna swing east or west right soon. You'll see. Might be figurin' to hole up in the Glass Mountains. Be able to swing from Pecos County to Brewster without much trouble. Seems like they're hittin' a faster pace, too. See them puffs of earth before an' behind each print?"

For two more hours the trail led south, south-west. The sun climbed higher, its rays grew more fiercely hot. Then abruptly the tracks swung dead south-west.

Pony George shot a look at Lawler. "Headin' fer the Bar-rillas, surer'n sin!"

Lawler nodded. "Right. Us, too. Barrillas ain't what you might call the property of Reeves County, but we're goin' there anyhow. I think we're gainin' a little, George. We may catch him by nightfall—sight him anyway."

"Bad business, fightin' in the dark," muttered Pony George. "Seems like we oughta give him more of a lead so's we'll come up with him to-morrer when there'll be plenty of light tuh line a sight with."

"We can't afford to give him any more of a lead than he's

117

already got. We're gettin' into buscadero country now. We gotta mind our P's an' Q's or some gent is goin' to tag us with a lead plum. We gotta get Link quick or we won't get him at all. Once his bunch gets holed up in them mountains they could hold us off for months mebbe. We gotta push on, George. Shake it up."

"I'll hev to agree with whatever you and yourself decide, I reckon," George said resignedly. "But it looks like tuh me these nags'd appreciate a little rest."

"We'll stop a spell in that grove of pig-locusts up ahead. Give us a chance to grab a bite an' the broncs can get their breath."

In a few minutes they pulled in beneath the shade of the twelve-foot trees Lawler had mentioned and pulled the saddles from their mounts. Lawler cuffed the dust from his clothes.

"Seems tuh me," Pony George mentioned between bites, "I heard there was a cantina round this stretch of cactus someplace. I could do with a spot o' likker."

Lawler's lips quirked queerly. "You're thinkin' of a place called the Saloon of the Hawk. It's a damned tough layout from all I've heard. Put up 'bout ten years back by a Mex breed. He's had his finger in every bit of deviltry inside a hundred miles ever since."

"Don't look like he'd get a whale of a lotta business round this stretch of hell," George commented. "Shouldn't think he'd get trade enough to pay fer haulin' his———"

"Don't say 'liquor', George," the sheriff cut in. "He makes his own, an' from what I've been told it's the sorta stuff that would make a grasshopper fight a curly wolf—an' lick him!" He gave his deputy a sidelong glance and chuckled. "Guess I'll buy you a coupla gallons."

Pony George snorted. "I hope yuh ain't figgerin' tuh compare me tuh no damn grasshopper! I'm a hard-tie man, by cripes, an' I won't take such talk from no man!"

The trail they presently followed twisted through many ravines and coulees as they pressed constantly into rougher country. Over hog-backs and eroded hills they went. On the rocky ridges which it crossed occasionally the trail became harder and harder to follow. Here Lawler's expert knowledge of reading sign stood them in good stead.

The sun's slanting rays cut down through a haze of dust stirred up by a vagrant breeze as the stifling afternoon wore along. Half an hour after their last conversation they lost the trail in the stony bottom of an arroyo. Right and left they cast looking for sign, but did not find it. Through the arroyo they finally pressed, hoping against hope to find tracks leading out of it. But the sandy ground outside yielded no faintest picture of riders having passed.

Lawler nodded grimly. "This," he said, "is it. I been expectin' for quite a spell they'd try somethin' like this. Link Holladay's no man's fool. We're wastin' time here, George. We could hunt from now till Kingdom Come an' not find a trail within three-four mile of here. We'll push on for that *El Gabilan* establishment."

"Now yuh're soundin'," Pony George approved. He wiped his streaming face with his dusty neckerchief. "Rest an' shade —beautiful shade—fer man an' beast, an' a drink fer ev'ry gent."

As they jogged along they noted abruptly the head and shoulders of a strange horseman coming over a distant rise. He saw them at the same time, but kept coming. They pulled up and waited. The stranger approached them slowly, hand raised in the peace sign.

There was a sparkle of braid on his fancy vest and, as Pony George remarked under his breath, "Looks like a dang potato bug—I mean uncommon gaudy."

. As he drew near, reining in a matter of twenty feet or so away, they saw him to be a broad-shouldered man with a stoop. His was a stubborn chin, Lawler noted, and a hawk's beak nose curled predatorily above his thin, trap-like lips. His piercing eyes rested on them with suspicion.

"Howdy," he drawled and smiled.

"Howdy," Lawler replied. He was glad he'd had the foresight to remove his badge some time ago. And glad that Pony George had done the same. To all intents and purposes, he and George were just a couple of drifting range hands.

"Thirsty weather," grunted Pony George. "Don't s'pose yuh know where we could get a drink, do yuh?"

The stranger's eyes swung to the deputy. "You pilgrims know anyone round this country?"

"No," answered Lawler, "we're just driftin' through. Might take a job of work if the pay looked right. You acquainted round here?"

"Wal, it's a swell country to drift through," the stranger's words were pointed.

"We'd rather get a job," said Lawler hesitantly. He had to be careful what he said and what sort of questions, if any, he put. These were trails seldom ridden by honest men—buscadero country where a throat could be slit for ten dollars up, and for nothing if one offended the inhabitants.

"Work's scarce in this man's country," returned the hawk-nosed stranger, gruffly. He tried to manoeuvre into a position from which he could get a look at the brands on their horses. But Lawler was not minded to have him do so, and shifted his own to match the other's movements. Pony George did likewise, cagily.

The stranger grinned, relaxing a little, and shot a questing look along their backtrail. "Don't see any dust cloud—yet."

"Was you expectin' to?" Lawler countered, playing up.

"Lots of gents sift through here with fellas raisin' dust behind 'em," said Hawk-Nose meaningly. "I take it you ain't that kind. So I won't tell you that I'm Hawk Bellero, what owns a cantina not far from here. Nor I won't be tellin' you that said place is two-three miles due west. What did you say yore handles was?"

Lawler growled, "We didn't say. But you can call me Redson an' my pardner's known as Han'some George—account he's so homely even a hoss-fly wouldn't look at him twice."

The stranger chuckled thinly. But not Pony George, who was touchy about his looks.

"Don't expect you could put us up for the night?"

"Don't reckon. But I might find a mite o' feed for yore nags."

"I could do with a long drink of somethin' that ain't got alkali in it," said Pony George with a gusty sigh. "I ain't the kind tuh enjoy these long fast rides."

Bellero shot him a glance and grinned. "Might be I could find a odd pint or two—if the price was right."

"I expect we could scrape up six-bits, mebbe, between us," Lawler said. At which Bellero laughed. It had a grating sound: was knowing. "Let's go," he said.

Turning their horses all three jogged due west, picking their way between the patches of prickly-pear, boulders and tall, yellow-stalked sotol adorning the surrounding landscape. Long cobalt shadows leaned down from the mountains and lapped across their path.

The vast silence of the country lay unbroken save for the soft thudding of the animals' hoofs until Bellero, after several covert glances at Lawler's inscrutable countenance, said casually:

"Must be quite a bit of excitement over Fort Stockton way since them two fellas held the stage up."

"Do you reckon?" Lawler's grin was satanic, so Bellero let it go at that.

*Chapter* **XXIII**

## TURPENTINE GULCH

HAWK BELLERO'S place was not by any means the only building in the little gulch where it was situated, the lawmen found when they arrived. But it was the largest of the group of shacks constructed from scanty timber and plenty of good tarred paper. It bore a sign above its door which read: SALLOON OF THE HAWK.

"What's the name of this place?" Lawler asked as the three stopped their horses before Bellero's cantina.

"Most folks in this man's country calls it 'town'," the hawk-nosed man replied. "But us that lives here calls 'er 'Turpentine'."

"Turpentine?" Pony George's jaw dropped. "That's a hell of a name to wish on a town. What's the idee?"

"Likely 'cause it's more'n average hot," Bellero grinned. "Most of the boys round here is gents of unkempt hair an' lightnin' draws. They got shifty habits an' itchy trigger-fingers. The name seems to fit us like a glove."

"Outlaw roost, eh?" Lawler scowled.

It was plain to him that Bellero regarded them as a couple of promising stage robbers, for he said soothingly, "Don't let that bother you. We're one big happy family, as the sayin' goes. All jolly good jaspers," he added gravely, "long as a man tends his own business an' don't show too much interest in his neighbours. You'll get along. You'll find my boys'll do tuh ride the river with."

Pony George muttered under his breath as Bellero dismounted, "I got a feelin' like a gol'fish in a bowl."

Bellero looked up and his steel-trap mouth quirked slightly at the corners. "We're all gentlemen here," he said. "We got a rule that keeps fellas from robbin' their compadres."

"Yeah, but what happens if some excitable gent forgets the rule?" asked George.

"He gets a hole dug for him the follerin' morning."

Lawler and Pony George dismounted and tied their horses to the long rack that fronted Bellero's saloon. Bellero then led the way inside.

The two lawmen beheld a long main room with a crude bar fixed up along one side. It was made with a rough plank and a couple of barrels. Behind it was a short shelf holding four big demijohns filled with an almost colourless liquid and alongside which were several labelled bottles. Along the opposite side of the room were six rough plank tables and a couple of dozen three-legged stools. At two of the tables a number of men were playing cards. That is, there were cards and money scattered on the tables, but the players were at the moment absorbed in a fight that was in progress in the centre of the room.

The two fighters did not appear very evenly matched and Queensbury rules had evidently been unheard of. One fighter was a big, brawny roughneck while his opponent was short and had a cast in one eye. But the short man seemed to be giving a good account of himself. Although his nose was bleeding and his good eye was shut tight, the big man looked as battered as though he'd been fighting six instead of the one puny fellow who crouched before him.

As Bellero and the two supposed stage-robbers entered, the hairy giant went back and down before a terrific crack from the blackjack held in the little man's right hand. He went down slowly, shaking his whiskered face from side to side as if to clear his head. There was blood drooling from his heavy lips.

"Now's yer chance, Pot-Eye!" shouted one of the gamblers. "Kick his damn face in!"

"That's about enough of that," said Bellero softly. "Lay off, Pot-Eye—you know the rules of my camp."

"Tuh hell with yer rules!" snarled the little man, and started for the fallen giant. He had one booted foot drawn back, preparatory to polishing off the fight in his own individual manner, when Bellero's right arm snapped forward in a short arc. A knife struck the little man hilt-first behind the ear. He went down and stayed down.

Bellero picked up his knife, returning it to the sheath inside his collar.

"Some of these boys are kind of slow in heedin' the rules," he apologised as two other men dragged the unconscious combatants outside. "But I teach 'em pretty fast, all things considered. Step up to the bar, gents, an' name yore favourites. This 'un will be on the house."

"Let's get outa here," muttered Pony George, nervously tugging at Lawler's arm. But Lawler ignored him, knowing it would be as much as their lives were worth to back down now. "We'll take whatever you recommend," he said.

Bellero stepped behind the bar and poured three glasses from the contents of a demijohn. They raised their glasses.

"To a short life an' a unknown grave," said Bellero.

When they set their glasses down empty, Pony George was still trying to get his breath. Several of the gamblers guffawed. "What'n time is this stuff?" demanded Pony George, huskily, when at last he found his voice. "Tobacco juice an' lightnin'?"

"Wal, that's comin' close enough. It's my own product," said Bellero modestly. "I got a secret process."

"Wal, don't never worry 'bout anyone tryin' to hook it," said Pony George, and felt tenderly of his lips.

After the two lawmen had eaten a passable supper at one of the smaller shacks, they returned to the saloon. Dusk was rapidly settling over the gulch and one or two stars were peering timidly forth from high above.

"This place ain't my idee of a good place tuh be," muttered George as they drew near the saloon. "Let's shove on 'fore we get shoved under."

"We'll stay to-night, anyhow," Lawler decided. "This is the best place we're like to hit for gettin' news of Holladay—or Tranton, either, if he's in the country. Keep your lip buttoned an' your ears skinned."

The saloon, they saw on entering, was crowded now. The gambling layouts were being patronised heavily; around one game the onlookers stood three deep.

A number of men were bellying the long plank bar. Lawler and Pony George sauntered toward it. Pony George regarded the demijohns dubiously.

"I'll try one of the bottles," he told the man in shirt sleeves who was serving as bartender.

"Me, too," Lawler spoke. He was aching to ask if any strangers had passed through recently but, being a stranger himself, knew that such a question would be distinctly out of order. It was necessary they move gently in this gulch of wanted men.

"I got a uncle and a girl cousin livin' in this country someplace," he said, as though to George. "You oughta meet the cousin—she's mighty easy on the eyes."

George looked blank but the barman grinned. "There ain't many," he said. "I reckon you're meanin' Sara——" He broke off as he caught a hard glance from the man next to Lawler.

"Frank," said this man coldly, "Dusty, down there, is waitin' tuh get served."

The loose-mouthed bartender took the hint and hurried off down the bar. The man who had cut short his conversation looked Lawler squarely in the eye. "Seems like I've seen yore face before somewheres. What did yuh say yore name was?"

"Redson—Flash Redson."

"Flash in the pan, I guess yuh mean, don't yuh?"

Lawler did not argue the point. His right fist whipped up in a mighty hook to the angle of the fellow's jaw. The belligerent one went over backwards and did not immediately rise.

The rattle of glasses and clink of coins abruptly hushed. Talk fell away as heads craned toward the lawmen. "Frank," said Lawler smoothly, "I'll take another glass of this tarant'la juice."

The room had grown very quiet, and in the stillness the sound of the barman's boots on the hardpacked ground seemed intensely loud as he came toward Lawler and thumped a pint bottle on the plank beside his glass.

Lawler gave him a grin as he poured a drink. Fishing a silver dollar from his pocket he laid it beside the bottle. Downing his drink and, followed nervously by Pony George, he headed for the door. The eyes of every man in the room, save those of the gent who still lay unconscious on the floor, seemed to be on his back. But——

"I think," he said casually, yet loud enough to be plainly heard, "we'll hunt up Bellero, George, an' have a little talk."

Some of these men, at least, had seen him and George enter with Bellero before supper, and Lawler was banking heavily that Bellero had not given out any information concerning them as yet. In which case he and George might be permitted to leave the saloon without further trouble.

Evidently such was the case for no overt move was made as they passed outside.

"Whew!" Pony George wiped his forehead on his dusty sleeve. "Me, I'm headin' outa this gulch fast as m' hoss will travel."

As they moved down the dusty lane that ran between the rows of tarpaper shacks, Lawler was glad as the deputy to be out again in the cool night air.

"Tell you what you do, George," he said softly as they paused. "I'm figurin' to stay a spell in spite of havin' had to knock down that suspicious gent. But I ain't figurin' to stay all night. You get your bronc an' fan dust. I got a hunch mebbe Sara an' Tranton are round here someplace. I'm goin' to try an' find out. You go to Toyahvale an' raise a posse; get a good-sized one if you can an' bust right back here. If you don't spare your horse you oughta make Toyahvale in two-three hours. Figure half an hour or so to get your men an' 'bout three hours to make it back here—that'll get you here round dawn. I'll try an' meet you outside town someplace." He gave George a shove. "On your way!"

As Pony George hurriedly vanished in the gloom Lawler, turning, saw another man coming toward him from the opposite direction; just a blurred bulk dimly discernible against the deeper black of the starlit night. There was no moon, for which the sheriff felt extremely thankful.

When the man came abreast, Lawler spoke. "Say, pard! Can

you tell a fella how to locate Bellero when he ain't in his bank?"

"Sure," said the other. "You must be kinda green round here. End shack. West end of the gulch," and off he jingled, headed toward the saloon Lawler had termed Bellero's bank.

"Further complications in the event of trouble," Lawler reflected grimly. "Me at one end of this town an' my horse at the other. This is gonna be no picnic if I have to make a run for it."

He thrust his big hands deep in his pockets, clamped his jaw determinedly and went striding along toward the shack the man had indicated. If possible, he meant to wring the information he was after out of Bellero—even if he had to do it at gunpoint.

He knocked when he reached the shack and Bellero's voice bade him in.

It was a much larger place, he found, than it had looked to be from the outside. He shut the door. There were two rooms, he saw; the second room opening off the wall across from that beside which the hawk-nosed boss of Turpentine was seated. Bellero peered up from the tally-book he had been examining.

"Howdy, Redson," he said, thrusting the book inside his coat. "Have a chair." For a time he sat regarding Lawler with his head on one side. Finally a slow grin quirked his lips. "Where's your pardner?"

"Left him buckin' the tiger," Lawler lied without hesitation. "I got in a quarrel with one of your boys an' decided the atmosphere in your saloon was not conducive to the Redson health. Thought I'd come up an' chin with you a spell."

Bellero grinned. "You don't wanta mind my boys. They're a little rough an' loud-spoken sometimes, but they mean all right. How d'yuh like my camp? Care tuh make it yore headquarters for a while?"

Lawler took plenty of time for his answer. This was delicate ground. "I ain't so crazy 'bout this camp," he replied slowly, "but I could get along with you first rate. I think you an' me could hit it off fine together. I'm aimin' to take a little pasear over the Barrillas in the mornin'. Got to see some gents. Small outfit run by a guy named Holladay. Don't s'pose you know him?"

"Holladay?" Bellero creased his brows. "Holladay—le's see, now. Seems like I've heard that name someplace." He squinted up at the ceiling poles reflectively.

"Dog-gone! You remind me that I *did* know a Holladay one time. Big, burly fella with fence-post legs an' a tight——"

"Was his name Link?" Lawler asked him swiftly.

"Yeah—his name was Link!" From behind the sheriff the words purred ominously across the silence. Lawler whirled.

Link Holladay stood gloating in the open door. A levelled gun was in his hand.

## Chapter XXIV

## THE WHEEL OF FORTUNE SPINS

LAWLER did not need anyone to tell him he was trapped; he knew it! If he chanced a draw, Death inevitably awaited him. He could not take but one of these outlaws with him, and there was no profit to him in that. If he stood motionless and allowed events to take their natural course the same end stood plain in view for him. Holladay grinned with his naked gun held ready. From behind his back came the grating chuckle of Bellero.

Lawler held his cheeks smooth, emotionless. He remained moveless, his massive shoulders hunched a trifle forward, his big hands hanging at his sides. He knew his danger fully yet no sign of fear marred the level directness of the glance he turned on Holladay. His eyes were like chilled jade.

Holladay's mocking lips framed a grin of triumph. "Gotcha!" he chuckled wickedly. "That damn coroner hit the nail plumb on the head, Lawler—you're too young an' tender green to ever be worth a row of shucks as sheriff. Hell, you're jest a damnfool kid!"

"I expect, Link, time will remedy that."

"Not in yore case it won't."

Lawler grinned easily. "Threatened men live long."

"Not the gents Link Holladay threatens. They got a habit of dyin' quick!"

"Yeah?"

"Yore hearin's good. This here's *my* camp you're in, young fella. We been drivin' rustled stock in here fer months. Hawk Bellero's boys takes a cut fer shovin' it crost the river."

"I can't see no sense," Bellero said, "spillin' yore guts to a sheriff."

"I'm doin' the talkin'," Holladay's tone grew ugly. "You an' me, Hawk, have got along so far because yuh had sense enough to mind yore own business. Keep on mindin' it or you'll wake up one o' these mornin's to find yoreself shovin' up daisies! Get his gun while I keep him covered."

Lawler, though his heart beat fast, offered no resistance

126

when Bellero reached round and lifted his Colt from its holster.

Holladay directed, "Better look him over fer a hide-out gun."

"He ain't got none," answered Bellero, patting Lawler up and down.

"All right. Take that flour sack over there an' tear it into strips an' tie his wrists behind him. Lash 'em good so's he can't even wriggle a finger."

Bellero did so; tying the knotted strips so tight they hurt. Yet Lawler was not noticing the pain. He was wondering if Pony George had gotten clear.

As though reading the sheriff's thoughts, Holladay grinned. "Don't figger too large on gettin' help from that clown depity of yores. I give the boys their instructions about *that* hairpin. By this time he's likely swingin' at a rope's end!"

Lawler's face remained unreadable.

"Set down on that stool over there," came Holladay's next command. "Jest one false move an' I'll bend this gun over yore scalp. Now *set!*"

Lawler, needless to say, sat.

"Hawk, tear up them other sacks." The burly rustler strode near to stand leering down at the trussed-up sheriff. "Wal, how do yuh like bein' the under-dog fer a change?"

Lawler made no reply, nor did his features express his feelings. He was watching the shadow of Bellero as the man tore flour sacks into strips. The shadow straightened. "Ready, Link."

"Lash his ankles to the legs of that stool. . . . Now run a coupla strips from his wrists underneath the seat an' then fasten the loose ends to his legs. There, that's fine," Holladay approved as Bellero finished his work and stood back. "If yuh get loose now it'll be by one of them there 'acts of Gawd'," he said with satisfaction.

Lawler saw scant likelihood of his getting loose. He wished now he had taken his chance on a gun battle, suicide though he had known it to be.

A rattle of shots went up from the far end of the street. He saw Holladay stiffen and felt Hawk Bellero go tense behind his back.

A startled curse fell from Holladay's lips as hurrying boots pounded near. He started to the door. Before he reached it, it was flung violently back against the wall. A wide-eyed man stood framed in the opening. He was breathing fast.

"Talk up!" snarled Holladay. "What's gone haywire now?"

"That blasted depity yuh told us tuh round up musta slipped away before we started huntin' him. We found that his nag was gone right off, but we figgered mebee he'd

127

moved it some place else, mebbe thinkin' tuh make a quick getaway. But we've searched the whole dang gulch an' neither the horse nor him is here!"

"What was that shootin'?" Holladay's tone was ominously quiet.

The man shivered. "Jest as we'd about concluded the depity had got away, Jed saw somethin' movin' in the shadows back of one of the shacks. He opened up an' so did the shadder. Jed went down, hit bad, clawin' at his stomach an' screechin' like a stuck pig! Me an' Ed an' Tanner joined in then an' got the fella, thinkin' it was that damn depity. But when we got a light an' went over there it was Bud Hennley we'd potted. There was six slugs through him an'——"

One blow of Holladay's gangling arm swept the speaker from the doorway. The next instant the burly rustler was outside and sprinting down the street. Lawler could hear the fast clump of his heavy boots. He grinned at Hawk Bellero.

"So George is gazin' at the stars from the end of a rope, eh?"

"You better sing low, Mister," Bellero said ominously, and turned to the man who had brought the news. "Go down an' keep an' eye on that girl. If she gets away the Chief'll have yore ears!"

After the man had gone Lawler grinned again at the scowling Bellero. "Better get on with your gut-shootin'. If Pony George gets to Toyahvale he'll have a posse back here before mornin'."

"If he does get through," Bellero snarled, "he won't be doin' *you* any good! The Chief'll fry *yore* bacon long before mornin'!"

Returning to his chair beside the wall Bellero sat down, not troubling to take his gun from leather. It would not be necessary and he knew it. He was too expert a thrower of the far-famed diamond hitch.

"If you got any prayin' tuh do," he pointed out pleasantly, "you better be gettin' on with it. Yore Sands of Time are due tuh run gosh-awful short."

From without the shack a soft *clink-clump* of spur rowels and high bootheels drew near. Again the door was flung open and Link Holladay came striding in, pushing before him a slender booted and belted figure that Lawler thought somehow familiar.

A girl in man's clothing! Lawler's cheeks went white as he saw her face.

"*Sara!*"

" 'Lo, Red. Going to join our happy family?"

Slim and virginal she stood before him. Yet staring at her Lawler felt a wave of fear grip him.

She seemed thinner now, more fragile than he remembered her. Her golden hair was a tangled mane. Her face was pale and there were deep, dark circles beneath her eyes. Yet these things but enhanced her beauty. It caused a hungry pounding of the sheriff's heart.

She faced him squarely; stood before his scrutiny with head uplifted, her eyes wide and level and unafraid. Whatever the hardships, the brutal contacts, she had been forced to undergo, they had not daunted her spirit. It burned in her eyes like a silver flame.

She spoke abruptly. "Red, I was wrong—terribly wrong. I thought——"

"Choke off the blat!" roughed Holladay. "Who cares what you thought? You got more damn lip than a muley cow!" And to Lawler: "Go on—look yore fill. She's *my* woman now, an she's gonna stay mine till I get sick of 'er an' find a better!"

Sara tautened; her dark eyes flashed.

"That's a lie!" she cried, and struck him with her open palm. "I never was your 'woman'!"

Holladay bent her a sweeping bow and chuckled at Lawler's futile anger. "Our Sara's a little wildcat. But I'll tame her—she's the kind I like in my string."

Sara darted to Lawler's side. Her stare at Holladay was defiant.

"Family tintype!" he jeered. "Make the most of it, m' dear, 'cause in a few hours you an' me'll be headin' for a nice long honeymoon in Manana Land." Then his mood abruptly changed; grew ugly. "Don't be gettin' so damn familiar," he rasped as Sara flung her arms about Lawler in sudden desperation. "I don't enjoy havin' my loot pawed over——"

"You won't enjoy havin' a rope around your neck, either!" Lawler gritted above her shoulder. "But I'll live to put one there."

Flecks of flame coalesced in Holladay's glare. He took a half step forward.

"Where's Tranton?"

Holladay's head went back in a mocking laugh. "You still huntin' *him?*"

A chill swept over Lawler as Sara pressed close against him. The chill was warranted.

"Hell, Tranton's been dead damn near a month," jeered Holladay. "I said you wasn't fit to be no sheriff—a gent with sense woulda figgered long ago that he wasn't the Pecos Killer!"

Lawler's startled glance swept Sara's face. "It's true," she said with trembling lip. "*I* thought Dad was the mysterious killer, too. So many little things seemed to——"

But Lawler was not listening. "Tranton . . . dead . . ."

"Sure he's dead," Holladay sneered, and then to Sara: "Go ahead. Tell the fool; he'd never learn no other way. What he learns now won't do him a heap of good, anyway. I'm settlin' his account."

Sara ignored him. "Some time before the killings started," she said to Lawler, "Holladay showed up. Dad seemed to change almost over night; he acted strange, uneasy, morose, abstracted. And then one night he told me he would be pleased if I married Link——"

Holladay's rough chuckle broke in on Sara's words.

Lawler's cheeks were grey beneath their bronze. He guessed what revelation was to follow and his square jaw clenched till the muscles stood out like ropes.

"To cut it short," Sara's tone was weary, "Dad said that Holladay was an old friend of his and I'd oblige him by marrying Link as soon as possible. He said he had a hunch it wouldn't be for long, and for that time in name only as I was to stay on the ranch. I could see that Link must have some fearful hold that needed time to break, so I married him. In Toyahvale—secretly. It was hard. But I couldn't let Dad down—he'd done so much for me.

"The next day the killings started. Dad and Holladay had a fearful row in Dad's office. I couldn't hear much of what was said. But I could tell that Dad was furious. After Link had gone he stayed in his office and wouldn't even come out for supper. The next few days he was gone most of the time. He never mentioned where he went but always came home late at night.

"Then one day I found some papers that had fallen from a pocket of his coat. They were things about the Toyah Lake gang—accounts. I guessed then that Dad was Rowdy Joe. Link had been a member, too. He had been hunting for Dad a long time——"

"That ain't no lie," Holladay growled. "When I found out where he'd been hidin' out I got in touch with the other boys an' put 'em wise. We fixed it up between us to get our splits or croak him. We drew lots an' I got the job of collectin'.

"I got my split right off. Tranton didn't want no trouble. He was gettin' along too well here. I told him if I got Sara I'd keep the other boys off. He finally saw the light. I reckon he was figgerin' to get me planted sudden but I kept outa his way.

"I sent for Doak an' when he showed I dropped Tranton a letter tellin' him to pay off quick or else. He paid—but swore to cook my goose." Holladay laughed. "He never saw

130

the day when he could outfigger me. I rubbed Doak out that night and pocketed his split."

"When I saw how nice it all worked out an' what a cinch it was, I wrote the other boys to start filterin' in an' I'd get their shares for 'em. I gave 'em the same share Doak got." Holladay sneered, "It was like takin' candy from a bunch of kids!"

"What was the idea of the 'Justice' notes?" Lawler asked.

"Just a red herrin' to throw folks off the trail. The gang thought Tranton was bumpin' 'em off. Reede got suspicious though. He was fixin' to clear out the night I stopped his clock. Them notes an' what follered 'em had scairt him pink. He'd just got one himself."

"What about Tawson?" Lawler was unable to keep the loathing from his voice.

Holladay sneered. "Tawson was jest damn fool enough to show he was gettin' wise. He figgered whoever was doin' the killin' would eventually get to Reede an' as he reckoned it was the Toyah Lake crowd gettin' rubbed out he played hands off, aimin' to nab the killer when he went for Reede. But he got to Reede's too late that night. The job was finished when he came."

An idea came to Lawler then. He asked, curious, "How about those shots at the Captain? That time he claimed someone had shot at him through the window?"

"I took those shots at him for a warnin'—he was threatenin' to kick over the traces an' spoil my show."

"All he had to do to wreck your plans," Lawler growled, "was to refuse to hand over the money you were supposed to be payin' them others."

"He didn't dare. He wasn't a heap anxious to get himself a harp. An' besides I told him I'd get Sara sure as hell if he didn't kick through."

"Why bother with those others, though? Why didn't you save time an' risk by forcin' the Captain to fork over all the loot at once?"

"No fun in that," Holladay explained, and laughed. "I aimed for him to see them others gettin' rubbed out one by one. He knew his time was comin', but I got a deal of pleasure outa keepin' him guessin' when. I tell you, I made them hombres sweat!

"Tranton knew what was goin' on, of course, from who laid the chunk. *But*—he couldn't figger no way of stoppin' it outside of killin' himself; I'd fixed things so that was the only out he had. An' he an' me both knew he'd never kill himself. He was too big a coward—had a yeller streak up his back three inches wide!"

"You mean," Sara corrected hotly, "that he was afraid to take his life for fear of what you might do to me!"

"Have it any way you want, m' dear," Holladay smirked and swaggered nearer to stand with arms akimbo, grinning down at Lawler. "Might's well quit gnashin' at the bit," he told the straining sheriff. "When I'm ready to pull stakes I'll see that yo're put outa yore misery. Until that time you might's well take it easy. You won't find no broken bottles, or handy knives, or jagged stones or tin around here to help you to get yoreself loose. You are pig-tied for slaughter, Sheriff, an' you might's well make up yore mind to it."

A wave of despair swept over Lawler. A keen appreciation of his helplessness was in him. This was to be the end—the end of all his plans and hopes and purposes. Desperately he forced his mind from such thoughts. He dare not contemplate the end with Sara in this renegade's power. Perhaps Pony George would get back in time with help . . .

"Bellero," Holladay's growl interrupted the sheriff's abstraction. "Get them boys of yores started off with the cattle. We're gonna have to quit this place 'fore that blasted depity gets back here with a posse. Get 'em started pronto! It's gettin' close to daylight. Sun-up ain't more'n one-two hours off."

Bellero rose and started for the door. "Think you can handle the filly?"

"You're damn well right I can! If there's any time Link Holladay can't hold his own against a female critter, it's time he was planted in his grave!"

With a chuckle Bellero left.

Holladay caught Sara by an arm; caught the other as she sought to strike him. "C'mon, yuh hellcat! Show sonny-boy Lawler how you kiss a real hard-tie man like yore lovin' husban'."

Her struggles suddenly infuriated him; letting go one arm he struck her across the face. In a twinkling he had both her wrists imprisoned in one big paw. He slid the other about her waist.

"C'mon, now—show 'im how you snuggle to yore Link!"

Lawler's jaws clenched hard. His sweat-beaded face was a lamplit mask as Sara put up a valiant but impotent struggle against the burly killer. Rage ripped through Lawler like jagged veins of fire; the room reeled redly before his eyes.

"Let go that girl, you swine!"

Holladay turned his head and leered.

"I'm gonna kill you like I would a snake," Lawler's words were thick with fury, "first minute I get loose!"

Tightening his grip on Sara's wrists, Holladay dragged her close to Lawler. "Yeah?" he jeered, and smashed his free fist into Lawler's chest with a force that sent him tumbling backward, stool and all.

"Yeah?" He swung a booted foot at Lawler's unprotected ribs—hard. A groan slipped through the sheriff's lips.

Sara kicked at Holladay's shins. With a snarl he flung her from him and again launched his booted foot at Lawler's side, more viciously than before.

But this time Lawler managed to roll sufficiently so that instead of thudding against his ribs, Holladay's blow caught one of the stool's legs and snapped it off clean! And that moment, out of the tail of his eye, the killer saw Sara making for the door. He went after her with a curse.

Lawler's pulse abruptly pounded; hope renewed surged through him like a heady wine. The lashings that bound him to the stool were loose! Link Holladay's brutal kick had proved a godsend!

Lawler worked one foot free and got to his feet with desperate haste. His wrists were still lashed behind him, but he could move—and that was something!

The debris of the stool lashed to one leg did not prevent him from limping toward where Holladay struggled with Sara beside the door. Yet just as he came within range the killer, catching the startled light that blazed uncontrollably in Sara's eyes, whirled.

One blow of Holladay's big fist sent the girl lurching across the room while his right hand dropped to his gun. With the weapon clearing leather Lawler's right foot, with the debris of the broken stool, came up in a smashing arc, struck Holladay's arm and sent the pistol spinning from his grasp.

With a smoking curse Holladay slammed his huge frame forward, both fists swinging. His rising right caught the sheriff full in the face. He brought his left in flush behind the sheriff's ear.

Lawler dropped.

Whirling, again Holladay made for Sara. But he brought up swiftly when he saw her hand was closing about his fallen gun. He dashed for the door, yanked it open. He went leaping through just as Sarah fired. The next moment he was gone from view.

Sara slammed the door and dropped its oaken bar in place. Crossing to Lawler's prostrate form she dropped to her knees beside him. Frantically she fumbled at the knots that held his wrists. He was conscious by the time she had the lashings off.

He struggled groggily to his knees. His head cleared swiftly as she worked to extricate his right foot from what was left of the wrecked stool. He commenced chafing his arms and wrists to dissipate the sensation of pins and needles coursing through them.

"Gosh . . . I—I don't know what to say," he stammered, embarrassed. "I—I—Sara, you're a brick!"

"You can save the compliments till we're out of this," she told him practically. "Here, take this gun and watch the window. Link Holladay won't be gone any longer than it will take him to get another pistol."

His mind was functioning more smoothly now. "Better put out that light," he whispered, as at last she freed his foot. "Hurry! His bunch may try to pick us off with rifles!"

With the room plunged in darkness Lawler's glance searched the sand beyond the window. There had been no moon and now the stars were not bright enough to dispel the heavy shadows that filled the outlaw gulch.

Sara stood beside him and when he realised it he slipped his arms about her hungrily and for a long moment held her tight. For that blissful interval of time her lips were pressed deliriously to his. The spell was broken when Sara freed herself at sound of running feet in the night outside.

With new life pouring through his arteries in a heavy tide, Lawler steadied the captured pistol on the window sill and waited.


## Chapter XXV

## POWDERSMOKE SHOWDOWN

THE sheer hopelessness of their position gradually absorbed the tonic of Sara's kiss; gloom again flooded Lawler's mind. To be sure, he had heard Hawk Bellero's men go off with the stolen stock and knew, therefore, there could be but few men left within the gulch. But even a few were like to prove several gents too many—especially as Link Holladay and Bellero both must be numbered among that few.

No moon shone down from heaven's blue bowl and the dying stars gave off but a sickly glow. False dawn's pale grey would soon be permeating the gulch. For such time was Lawler waiting, yet he knew the outlaws would strike before.

Black shadows filled the shack. Muffled whispers drifted in through the open glassless window. Lawler's eyes, keened by many a night hunt, saw a flitting shadow cross a lighter space somewhere between the shack and Hawk's saloon. A grim smile crossed his lips. He had no lead to waste; each shot must be made to count.

A wind had sprung up and Lawler, his nerves strung taut, could hear the dismal swishing of the sage and rabbitbrush. Sara huddled against him, shivering.

"Red!" she suddenly clutched his arm. *"Red!"* there was hysteria in her voice. "We can't stay here! They'll burn us out! These tarpaper walls are no protection! They'll blaze like tow! *Quick*—unbar the door!"

"Sara!" he shook her roughly. "Come out of it! You can't let go like that!"

She started to scream. He saw it coming and dropped his pistol on the sill to clamp one hand across her mouth. She tried to bite and he slapped her sharply across the cheeks with his free hand. "Stop it! Get hold of yourself, Sara!"

He could feel her shaking in his grip. He shook her fiercely. "Stop it!"

"I—I'm all right now, Red. I'll behave," she told him huskily.

Releasing her, Lawler felt for his pistol on the sill. Feverishly his hand swept it from end to end three times before he would let himself believe that it was gone. Then, the implications of the fact breaking over him, he softly swore.

"What is it, Red?"

"My gun—it's gone. I must have dropped it out the window. I'm gonna climb through after it. We wouldn't have a chance without a gun." He did not think they had a chance anyway, but could not bring himself to tell her so for fear she'd realize she was hampering his movements. "Down on the floor now. Quick," he muttered, "them birds may open up any second. I don't want you hit!"

"Don't leave me, Red!" Sara cried as he thrust a leg across the sill. "Please—I couldn't bear to lose you now . . ."

"Don't be silly! I gotta get that gun!"

"Red, please—"

"Git down!" he growled, and dropped to the ground outside. Almost instantly one groping hand came in contact with the cold steel of the errant pistol. As he picked it up a spur rowel clinked against a stone. A burst of flame sheered the mark to his right and lead splashed whining off the rock!

Motionless Lawler crouched there. He did not dare return the unknown's lead for fear of drawing a leaden hail upon the shack. Bullets would sail through those flimsy walls like cardboard—and Sara was inside.

A little hush closed down; a stillness far more sinister and disturbing than ever could be the natural silence of this land. It seemed as if the entire world were waiting breathless.

With infinite caution he slowly straightened. For long moments he stood there motionless, one more shadow among the multitude. Then swiftly thrusting a leg across the sill, he pulled himself inside and drew the other leg in after him.

Something was wrong—*he knew it instantly!* What it was he could not tell, but something— Danger cocked his muscles, held his big frame tense. Then his voice crossed the silence recklessly:

"*Sara!*"

He knew then what was wrong. No answer came, yet he sensed a stirring of the shadows by the door leading into the back room. He dropped to the floor so he would not be silhouetted against the window's lesser gloom.

Something had happened to Sara while he'd been outside. That back room must also hold an exit from the shack! Someone had entered this place——

A faint scuffling came from the deepest shadows across the room. Lawler drew back the hammer of his pistol to full cock. In the strained hush the sound was like the striking of a gong! Tense, he drove his voice across the darkness:

"*Who's there?*"

Came a faint creak of leather, a *swish-h-h!* and something that even in this murky light gleamed dully slithered past his cheek and struck the wall behind with a sharp *thwunk!*

A knife! Hawk Bellero was across the room!

Lawler flattened—and just in time! A streak of flame speared out above him. He worked his trigger feverishly, angling his shots upward into the clustered shadows near the back room door. Dimly in the thunder he caught Bellero's ripped-out curse and knew one shot at least had scored. Then came the thud of bootheels crossing the back room floor. A cold dank silence crept shivering back as sounds of his shots dimmed out.

Fumbling in the gloom Lawler shoved fresh cartridges into the emptied chambers of his smoking gun. Then, despite the crazy danger of the thing, he struck a match. Bursting orange against the wavering shadows it showed an empty room. Bellero, if Bellero it was, had gone.

The man would not be fool enough to linger now in that back room, so Lawler did not look. He dropped the match into the pile of discarded flour sacks from which Bellero had torn the strips to lash him, scooped the igniting material against a wall. He watched for a moment while the yellow flames licked up. Then—pulling the bar from the door—he slid outside.

Sprinting thirty crouching feet he dropped behind a clump of sage.

The tarpaper shack burned with a fiercely wild abandon; the red-tipped flames licked up its flimsy walls with hissing fury. For a hundred yards the towering blaze lit up the surrounding earth as bright as noonday, picking out each stump and bush with crystal clarity.

Lawler, belly-down behind his bit of sage, waited with levelled pistol, his narrowed glance probing the brightened area in searching stabs.

Abruptly his vigilance received reward. A man bounding up from a nearby thicket commenced to run. He was headed for the shadows bulking large beyond the radius of the flames.

"Halt!" snapped Lawler grimly. But the man ran on unheeding. Maliciously Lawler's finger squeezed the trigger of his levelled gun, relaxed when the runner, clutching wildly at his side, spun half around and went to his hands and knees. A moment he swayed there crazily in the fireglow, then pitched suddenly forward on his face.

"One," Lawler said deliberately.

Not far to his left a man jumped swiftly to his feet and whipped a rifle to his shoulder. Flame belched instantly from its muzzle; whining lead cut twigs from the bending sage.

"Close," Lawler grunted, and let the hammer drop again. The man with the rifle went over backward, sprawled motionless against the yellow earth in the light of the leaping flames.

"Two," said Lawler grimly, and replaced the spent shells with fresh ones from his belt. "These polecats will soon learn they're pawns in a damn bad game!"

At the dim edge of the firelit circle nearest the Hawk's saloon, Bellero sprang from his place of concealment. He went dashing toward the saloon, unnerved by what he had seen.

Knowing the distance far too great for accurate pistol work, particularly in the present circumstances Lawler held his fire and went plunging after the fleeing outlaw. It was in the sheriff's mind that if he could keep the fellow in sight, Bellero would probably lead him to Holladay and the girl.

He yelled at the rustler to stop. Bellero did—but only to turn and fire. His lead went harmlessly overhead and to the side due to his hurried aim and, seeing Lawler cutting down the distance, he turned and ran again. Ran until he reached the corner of a shack, round which he dashed with unabated speed.

As Lawler drew near the spot he slackened pace. It was darker here and Bellero might be lurking round the corner hoping for a finishing shot. Lawler stopped and listened. But he heard no sound save the crackling of the flames behind.

Crouching lower against the earth he worked cautiously closer to the place where the Hawk had vanished. He wanted to angle out so as to command a view of that hidden corner before coming too near. But to do so would bring him uncomfortably close to the adjacent shack. And Holladay might be laying for him there.

He caught abruptly a blur of movement and there was Bellero crouched before him in the open.

"This is *it!*" the hawk-nosed outlaw snarled, and a burst of flame belched outward from his levelled gun.

Even as Lawler hurled himself aside, from the tail of one eye he saw a second crouching figure rock into view from round the corner of the opposite shack.

Shot upon shot choked the gulch with smashing echoes. Lead ripped through the brush back of Lawler in a thumping hail of sound. A blow rocked against his head and he felt himself sagging as red flame and whirling lights danced pinwheel-like across his vision. He staggered and went down, the gun in his hand still spitting.

But consciousness did not leave him. He got his chin up on a fist and saw Bellero slumping down against a shack. A red mist swam before his eyes yet did not obscure Holladay's burly form lumbering toward him through the half light, big pistol gripped in hairy paw.

Pulses slowing Lawler fumbled with the cartridges in his belt, striving doggedly to jam fresh ones into the empty cylinder of his gun. He knew that the end had come yet inside him something whispered that he was glad it was to be like this. Though he died for it, he was glad to be here now facing Link across levelled guns.

Wiping the blood from his eyes he struggled to his knees. The pain the effort cost him was excruciating yet he managed to lurch erect. "Come an' get it, polecat," he whispered.

Holladay lumbered closer, watching his enemy through slitted lids. With twenty feet separating them, light from the burning shack picked out his snarling features—showed blood drolling from his mouth.

There was something fierce and blazing in the outlaw's slitted eyes. Whether it was jealousy, hate or envy Lawler could not tell; perhaps it was none of these, or a mixture of them all. But there was unswervable stubbornness in the forward throw of his jaw.

Lawler's gun hand hung at his side. "Say when," he whispered hoarsely.

"*Now!*" cursed Holladay, and his pistol rose in a bursting arc of flame.

With lead tearing through his hat Lawler's gun bucked his palm in sharp recoil—just once.

Features twisting with incredulity and rage Holladay's forward lurch abruptly stopped. His thin lips writhed back from his great yellow teeth in a savage snarl. His yellow neckerchief grew red in the firelight as he stood there swaying,

138

trying again to work the trigger of his gun. He swore thick drooling oaths when his failing muscles refused the dictates of his stubborn will.

Swiftly then his twisted features reflected the ghastly realization that he was done, was dying on his feet—was shuffling as he'd shuffled others. His legs let go at the knees and pitched him forward on his chest, shoved his face in the yellow dust. Limp and motionless he lay there, one arm outflung, the other crumpled under him.

This much Lawler saw, and then the world blacked out to the drum of approaching hoofs.

He came reluctantly back to a world made noisy by stamping feet and shouting voices. His head throbbed as though he'd bumped it on some rafter. His body burned with shooting, fiery veins of flame. Some damned fool seemed to be hammering a dull knife into his shoulder and turning it round and round.

Gentle hands now were turning him over. One cool hand was smoothing back the red hair from his forehead. It was soft and cool, that hand, and soothing. He felt grateful for its touch and, wondering whose it was, opened his eyes. He shut them almost instantly for he was in some place that was bright with light—sunlight!

After a time the sound of voices and other noises became more distant. He ventured to open his eyes again. He did so, tensing. Hair like spun gold framed a familiar face above him—it was like the face of someone he had known in the distant past. Then realization came flooding back to him. This was the inside of a shack in Turpentine Gulch—*it was Sara's face above him!*

"Sara!"

"Red—I'm so glad!"

He could see now there were tears in Sara's eyes. Oblivious to the pain that racked his bruised and battered body, Lawler struggled to a sitting posture beside her and, slipping his good right arm about her, drew her close.

"It's all over, hon," he whispered with his lips against her hair. "Link Holladay is dead."

She nodded, hid her face against his chest and sobbed. He saw his ring upon her finger and guessed with quickening pulse she must have got it from his pocket. It gave him courage to say:

"Soon's we get back to town we're gettin' married, Sara."

"You wouldn't want to marry the daughter of Rowdy Joe——"

"Reckon you don't know much about me then—I can't think of anythin' that would please me better. I——"

He broke off as boots with chiming spurs came creaking

139

up. A nearby door popped open and a long swift ray of sunlight sped across the floor and then was blotted by a shadow as a man stopped in the opening. He had a drawling nasal voice and used it now to say:

"Wal! Wal! I was gonna make a report to—but shucks, m' boss Red Lawler wouldn't be found in no place like this here! 'Seems like I've done busted into the ward for the incurably romantic——"

"That ain't funny, George," said Lawler, as Sara snuggled closer.

"Wal, cripes!" said Pony George, "even Homer was knowed tuh nod!"

**THE END**

**Nelson Nye** was born in Chicago, Illinois. He was educated in schools in Ohio and Massachusetts and attended the Cincinnati Art Academy. His early journalism experience was writing publicity releases and book reviews for the *Cincinnati Times-Star* and the *Buffalo Evening News*. In 1935 he began working as a ranch hand in Texas and California and became an expert on breeding quarter horses on his own ranch outside Tucson, Arizona. Much of this love for horses can be found in exceptional novels such as *Wild Horse Shorty* and *Blood of Kings*. He published his first Western short story in *Thrilling Western* and his first Western novel in 1936. He continued from then on to write prolifically, both under his own name and the bylines Drake C. Denver and Clem Colt. During the Second World War, he served with the U.S. Army Field Artillery. In 1949–1952 he worked as horse editor for *Texas Livestock Journal*. He was one of the founding members of the Western Writers of America in 1953 and served twice as its president. His first Golden Spur Award from the Western Writers of America came to him for best Western reviewer and critic in 1954. In 1958–1962 he was frontier fiction reviewer for the *New York Times Book Review*. His second Golden Spur came for his novel *Long Run*. His virtues as an author of Western fiction include a tremendous sense of authenticity, an ability to keep the pace of a story from ever lagging, and a fecund inventiveness for plot twists and situations. Some of his finest novels have had off-trail protagonists such as *The Barber of Tubac*, and both *Not Grass Alone* and *Strawberry Roan* are notable for their outstanding female characters. His books have sold over 50,000,000 copies worldwide and have been translated into the principal European languages. The *Los Angeles Times* once praised him for his "marvelous lingo, salty humor, and real characters." Above all, a Nye Western possesses a vital energy that is both propulsive and persuasive.